PAINTING WITH FIRE

K.B. Jensen

DEDICATION

This book is dedicated to my wonderful husband, my ocean.
Thank you for putting up with all my daydreaming and helping
turn this book into a reality.

PROLOGUE

Steve Jackson was trying to get his Honda Civic through the snow, but the tires spun loudly and the vehicle wouldn't swim through. "Come on baby, please, please, we need to get out of here now," he coaxed and swore.

But the Civic couldn't climb out. It slid back into its final resting place, crooked against the curb. He turned off the ignition and slumped forward with his gloved hands on the wheel and his forehead against the top of it. He felt drained, empty. He had said what he needed to say and it wasn't wise to linger. They let him walk out the door but they could still change their minds.

"Thank you, God, it's over," he said. "Now, please help me get the hell out of here."

He was surprised they hadn't stopped him after he gave his "notice." Drug dealers aren't normally so courteous. They don't give you a card and a goodbye lunch before you walk out the door. But the worst of it was over now and he just had to drive home in the storm.

Blinking the snow out of his eyes, he glanced up at the old, three-story brick building through the blur of snowflakes and saw a dark face in the oversized window. It moved back behind the curtain.

He got out of the car and started digging out holes behind

the tires, kicking the snow with his boots. He shivered. He was only wearing a puffy black vest over a flannel shirt. He had been too preoccupied to listen to the forecast that morning, too nervous about getting killed to worry about what clothes he'd be wearing when the shots would ring out. Snow had been the last thing on his mind when he showed up to tell them he couldn't work for them anymore. His conscience wouldn't allow it, that feeling in the pit of his stomach every time he made a delivery. A 13-year-old girl had thanked him, for what? For helping her kill herself slowly. He knew he had to answer to God one day and the day was coming soon, sooner than he'd like.

He bent down and dug out the snow with his gloved hands. The blur of white snowflakes stung his eyes so he could barely see. He didn't hear the footsteps in the snow behind him through the whistle of the wind. He didn't hear the metal slide through the air as it sliced down and cracked open the top of his head. He spun sideways from the blow and fell.

For a matter of seconds, he lay there flat on his back in the snow bank watching the flakes twirl and land on his face. His vision whirled. He had bitten his tongue, but he could still taste the snow melt and mix with blood as it dropped into his open, gurgling mouth. He thought of his mother, what she would say when she found out? Did she know that he had changed? She'd never know.

"Jesus," he gurgled. It was a prayer this time.

Then the heavy metal blade came down again, and the white out turned to a permanent black out.

1 THE VIEW

The radiator pipes were like the coils of an albino viper. They hissed, bitingly hot. White, cracked paint peeled off the iron like an old set of skin. The boiling air bent as it wafted out of the open window. Claudia and Tom sat in sweat, wondering when it would turn off, praying in 95 degrees for an end.

"We pay too much for this apartment," Tom said. "The vintage vibe is overrated, and the neighbors suck. I've got a bad feeling this neighborhood is only going to get worse, too."

Claudia pulled her thick, dark brown hair back away from the base of her moist neck and then let it fall back down.

"If I move, I'm part of the problem," she said. "I'm not moving. You're sweet to stay, but you don't have to, if you don't want to. I'm a big girl. I'll figure it out."

"Sure, so you're gonna magically pay the rent without a job? Would you really be OK without me?" he asked.

He shrugged like he didn't care, but Claudia could see the slump in his shoulders.

"That's not what I meant. I wouldn't be better off, but you might be," Claudia said. "I just want you to know you don't owe me anything. You know, it's nice having you here. I like living with an artist."

"I work retail, Claude," he rolled his eyes.

"You're going to make it one day," she said. "I'm not the only one who loves your work, am I? Are you saying I have bad taste in men and art?"

He laughed. A strange irony was that when he first moved in, he was the unemployed one without any money. Claudia had been looking for a roommate in any case, but he was the one without a job at the time. The only thing he had to offer was his artwork. It hung all over the apartment walls, images of old buildings, lost architectural relics, and women in white walking on the beach in shimmering silver moonlight. He had a strange monochromatic style where he would pick one color and just run with it, shades of purple and black, shades of red and black, silver, gold, shades of orange.

Lately, she had noticed more than a few canvases draped in white sheets in his room. It made her uneasy, like he was hiding something. There was also something unsettling about waking up on the couch only to find him hastily putting his pencil and sketchbook away, like she had caught him doing something dirty. Why was he so secretive about his art, she wondered. Were all artists like this?

Claudia thought of saying more. She reached over and touched the damp, bare skin of his arm lightly then pulled her hand back. After four months of sharing the same apartment, she still didn't know him that well.

There was always something he kept hidden away. When he first moved in, she had asked him about his past and he had responded with clipped answers to her questions about where he was from, his childhood, even his art.

"Where did you learn to paint so well?" she had asked him once.

He had paused a long time and then finally answered. "I took some courses."

He gave her a handful of words and a thousand images. His paintings covered every inch of the walls. He had no problem expressing himself in paint. But if she asked him what a painting meant, he would always ask her to find her own meaning. It was both a fun game and frustrating one.

Tom was nothing else if not highly entertaining, she thought.

He tapped his fingers against the arm of the couch. The sound brought her back to the present.

He was shirtless. Claudia was so used to it she didn't notice it much anymore, except when the neighbors knocked on the door. She tried not to notice anyway. Things could get awkward, but maybe it would be a good thing if things got awkward, she thought. The neighbors must've thought it was odd to be greeted by a chestful of hair at eye level when he swung open the door, but with the heat blasting out the radiators she was sure they understood the dilemma. Tom was just over six feet and almost Mediterranean looking, in a classic dark sort of way.

"I'm grateful," she said. "I'll find a job soon. I promise. But after I do, you don't have to stay here if you don't want to. You can find a nice place on your own. You don't owe me anything anymore."

"Yeah, I do, Claude. And I love the light in this place," he said, his dark brown eyes shifting away from hers and up toward the ceiling and around the room. The silhouettes of tree branches danced across the sun-streaked walls.

"But I don't like the radiator heat," he added. "Or the neighbors fighting next door."

"I'll open another window." she leaned forward to get up and the skin on her lower back peeled off the sticky leather couch, from the gap between her sweaty tank top and jeans.

Looking down at the dirty snow banks below, from the window, she saw something strange sticking out of the freshly fallen snow – fabric and a small something, grayish blue.

"Christ," she said. "That's not what I think it is, is it?"

Tom came to peek over her shoulder, three stories down into the wintry lunar-like landscape.

"It looks like a sleeve, part of an old flannel shirt." He breathed on her neck. "Someone must have tossed it on the ground or dropped it."

"I don't think it's just a shirt." Claudia squinted. She inhaled sharply and couldn't seem to let go of the breath.

Her face turned pale. "What if there's more under the snow? I'm going down there."

"It's not like it's moving. You're paranoid," Tom said, but he tossed on a shirt and followed her to the closet where they bundled up in wool coats and hats.

"It's not right," Claudia said. "It's almost like an outline of…" Her voice trailed off shakily. Maybe the neighborhood kids were playing tricks on her.

"Since when did you have laser vision?" Tom said. "I didn't see anything besides a shirt."

She buttoned up her jacket in the old, dimly lit stairway. Then she bolted downstairs with a series of quick, frantic thuds. Her boots kicked up a haze of musty dust, emanating from the blue, floral carpet snaking down the wooden steps.

"You're just imagining things." Tom shouted as he trailed slowly behind her down the three flights. He let his fingers slide slowly down the long wooden banister. "I'm sure it's nothing, just a reflection on the snow."

"I don't think so!" she shouted, the panic rising in her voice.

She thudded down the last marble steps, swung out the double doors in front of the building and ran to the corner behind the bushes, kicking up puffs of snow behind each step. There in the snow bank, she saw the flannel sleeve and something sticking up slightly out of the melting snow – a bluish white thumb. She sank to her knees and Tom ran up behind her.

"Holy shit," he said, his voice shaking. "Don't touch it."

"What if he's still alive?" she said.

In shock, Claudia's fingers reached out and felt the frozen hand beneath the snow. Her fingers curled backward and immediately started to shake. She could still feel the hard, frozen hand. The rest of the body was buried under the snow. She dug out his face and recoiled.

"Fuck, shit, shit," poured out of her mouth as she tried to dial the police on her cell phone. Her fingers kept hitting the wrong numbers and the phone crackled in and out as she yelled at the dispatcher trying to tell them which corner they were on and what they had found.

"Police are on the way. We'll send an ambulance," the woman's calm voice answered.

"But he's dead, he's dead," she said, gasping in the cold air. She hung up the phone and repeated the words. "He's dead, Tom. He's dead."

"It will be ok," he said.

They stood there for a few minutes waiting for the wail of the sirens and staring down at the body.

The frozen, glass-like eyes and solid blue lips were parted as if he were about to whisper something from another world. A frozen, red-crusted wound crowned the top of his head. Claudia started to cry and Tom put his arms around her.

"It's ok, it will be ok," he said, swallowing uneasily. "Maybe it was an accident."

"I don't think, so," she said, sobbing into his wool coat. "Just look at him."

Two squad cars slid up in front of the building and Tom backed away as four officers poured out and ran toward the front door, slamming the doors behind them. They left their squad cars running, coughing up hot, gray exhaust into the cold air.

"They'll think we did it. Shit." Tom suddenly looked like he was about to run.

"No, they won't," Claudia said and grabbed his arm. "Why would they? Over here!"

An officer leaned his husky frame over the snow bank and looked down. He pulled up the collar of his black coat.

"Damn it. The eighth body this year and it's only January," he said.

His colleagues unfurled the yellow tape.

"I'm Detective Stan Hughes," he said, shaking their hands. "Did you see what happened?"

"No," Claudia said. "I just saw him out the window."

They shook their heads and the officer pulled them down the street about 20 feet away from the body and took out his notepad.

"Any idea who did this?" he asked Claudia.

"No idea." She said. She stared at his badge.

"Ever see the guy before?"

"No."

"Darling," he said, patting her on the arm. "Any information you might have that would be helpful?"

"Not really," she said, sniffling.

Stan breathed on his fingers and wrote down her name and information on his notepad.

Claudia's jeans were cold and stiff. She tried to brush off the snow with her numb fingers, but it had melted in patches across her legs, cracked and crinkled into the denim folds.

"Any people you know around here who might do something like this?"

"I don't know," she said. "The neighbors next door get into loud fights, but I don't know that that means anything."

"What kind of fights?" he asked.

"Nasty ones," Tom interjected. "The two of them are always screaming, knocking shit over and we hear loud thumps and things falling on the other side of the wall. It's fucking annoying."

"Do you call us?"

"No," Tom said.

"Why not?" Stan said. "How're we supposed to fix a problem we don't know about? What if he kills his wife and you don't call?"

"I didn't think you guys really cared about loud noises," Tom said.

"We care," Stan said loudly. "We always care. Next time, you call me." He handed them his cards.

"Were they making any noise yesterday or today?"

"No," Claudia said.

"What were you two doing last night?"

"Sleeping," Tom said.

"Me too," Claudia said.

"No big plans for a Friday night?" Stan said. "You two are a lively couple."

"We're not a couple," Claudia said.

"So you were sleeping alone last night," Stan said.

"Yes," Claudia said.

"Ok then," he said and scribbled something down on his notepad. Tom gave Claudia a worried look.

She turned and watched the coroner's white van pull up. On the side were the cheerful words, "It's about life, not death." What a lie, Claudia thought. She watched a man pull out a stretcher from the back. A camera swung from his neck.

"Looks like a blunt instrument hit him," the man said to his colleague. "Quieter than a gunshot."

Claudia tried not to look anymore as they went to load the body. She didn't want to see the dead man's face again, but she couldn't seem to help looking. They pulled a sheet over the body, but it didn't make her feel any better.

To block her from the view, Stan stepped in front of her and pulled out a cigarette. It didn't matter, but she wondered what ethnicity he was. His skin was light enough that he could've been mixed. He had light brown eyes and short, cropped, black hair. Claudia thought he was good looking for a man in his 40s. His breath came out in a mist mingled with warm smoke.

She watched him hold his cigarette. Her hands ached to curl around the burning end just for the warmth. She kept shoving them into her pockets but there was no sensation left in them. The feeling of the dead man's fingers lingered there but nothing else. She had shaken hands with a dead man, she thought with another shiver. Claudia tried to breathe on her hands and rub them to warm them up, but she couldn't. She wondered if they'd stay cold forever.

"God, I wish I had seen something," she said, shivering.

"Well, someone must have last night," he said, putting out his cigarette in the snow. "The question is whether they'll talk. That's always the question, my dear."

"I'm not so sure about that," Tom said, putting his arm around Claudia. "It was snowing pretty hard last night. I couldn't see a damn thing outside last night when I looked out the window."

Tom pulled her away from Stan and the two of them walked back into the building.

"Not much of an alibi you gave him," Tom whispered harshly as soon as they closed the front door. "You should have told him we were together."

"I wasn't aware we were suspects," Claudia said.

"Of course we are," Tom said. "Who isn't after something like that?"

"They've got no reason to think I did it," Claudia said. "Why? Do they have a reason to suspect you, Tom?"

"No," he said loudly. He turned his back to her and thudded up the stairs.

"I mean, it's not like we're criminals or anything," she shouted after him.

Tom said nothing in response, just fumbled with the doorknob and swung open the door back into the heat. She felt heavy as she walked up behind him. The silence was not a reassuring answer.

2 TORN PAPER HEARTS

Within 24 hours of the body being found, the view from outside the old, oversized window had almost gone back to normal. The neighboring residents were back to their routine lives, driving off to work and walking to the train. They scurried down below in the snow with their black and brown coats, and their scarves wrapped around their mouths. Foot tracks crisscrossed the snow banks and a depression in the snow showed where the body had been dug out. But all that looked like a blank gray white canvas from the third floor looking down. Claudia kept compulsively checking the window. Did it really happen? There was no one to talk to about it. She had pulled up a chair and tied back the curtain. She couldn't seem to sit still. She kept getting up and sitting back down, checking the window.

Tom had driven her car to his day job. He was a cashier at a big-box retailer ten miles away. He called it an "evil, soulless corporation," but the job paid the rent and supported his art habit. Occasionally, he sold something. Claudia wished she could say the same. It hadn't always been this way. After dropping out of college, she had worked for a bookstore for five years before she was laid off. Sometimes, she thought about going back to school, but she couldn't seem to decide what she wanted to do.

Hours passed and she looked out the window again and noticed something had changed in the landscape. She stared out the window at seven people down below. She couldn't see their faces, just the tops of their hats and their puffy winter coats hobbling below. Two were children with their heads bowed down. Claudia kept going to the window and looking out at them. They were standing right in the snow where the body was found, paying their respects.

Finally, she sat down on the couch and tried to watch TV instead. It was a soap opera in overdramatic Spanish that she didn't really understand. She watched the women's mouths move and tried to guess what they were yelling about under all that red lipstick. Maybe it was something about the crying baby. She suspected it was the same old plot about the baby who was swapped at birth. The mother was told the child died, but it was a lie. Of course, it would probably take months for the truth to slowly unfold on screen and she would never really know for sure what they were saying, what was really happening.

She wondered about the soap opera down below. Claudia wanted to know what was going on since she found the man, but she didn't want to intrude. It was none of her business who his family was or what they thought about it.

She kept pulling out the clunky, black laptop and rereading the news story on the fingerprint-streaked screen. The words may as well have been in Spanish. There was so little detail to the story. The man's name was Steve Jackson. The coroner ruled his death a homicide with blunt-force trauma to the head.

Police were still looking for a suspect. She couldn't stop thinking about it. Would they ever know why he was killed? She flipped the laptop shut and put it down on the table. The computer started to hum a loud, angry whirling sound, like it was about to burst into flames.

She put on her jacket and hat. She hesitated on her way down the stairs but kept her feet moving. She just wanted to talk to someone.

A death notice had been put up at the entrance of the

building, just like the notices they put up when they turn off the water for a few hours. It told the time and date of the wake and funeral. It made the whole thing feel so mundane.

Outside, the children tied paper hearts to the bushes with words written on them. "Goodbye, Uncle Steve. We'll miss you. RIP." One of the paper hearts had already been ripped apart by the winter wind.

An old woman stared numbly at the half-melted snow bank, looking for something that wasn't there.

"I'm sorry for your loss," Claudia said softly.

"I always knew I'd lose him," she mumbled. "Are you the one who found him?"

"Yes." Claudia swallowed a gulp of cold air.

"Thanks," she said softly. "I'm his momma. I always thought the drugs would get him, but not like this. He's a sweet boy. He's trying to change. He was going to a new church, praying to God for help. He planted flowers in my yard last summer. But the wrong people. He just kept seeing the wrong damn people."

The words flooded out of her. Claudia couldn't help but notice the present tense, like Steve wasn't really dead yet to his mother. Understandably, her mind hadn't yet wrapped itself completely around the fact. Claudia found herself patting her on the shoulder, not sure if she should hug her or retreat back up the stairs.

"Is there anything I can do to help?" she asked.

"Not unless you can find the person who did this," she muttered. "I pray that he finds Jesus."

"Lord help him if I find him first," the man next to her said. Faint blue circles lined his bloodshot eyes and Claudia could smell the beer on his breath.

The dead man's mama sobbed. Claudia didn't know what to do. She hugged her and cried with her. Through the thick downy layers of a winter coat, she could feel the woman's small frame shaking in a shuddering mixture of anger and grief. She could feel the frozen tears against her cheek, mingling with her own.

"Thanks for finding my boy," she said. "Are you coming to the funeral?"

"I'm not sure," Claudia said, wiping her eyes. "Should I?"

She wrapped her red scarf tighter around her neck and over her mouth. It hurt to breathe the same cold air. It was a relief to march back up to the hissing radiator heat upstairs. The pipes were banging.

She cast off the wool jacket onto the floor. She unwound the scarf from around her neck and rubbed her throat. Then she sat down on the couch. She wished Tom were there so she could rest her head on his shoulder and tell him all about it. Instead, with it all still trapped inside her, taking short, tight breaths, she turned the TV back on and tried to forget.

It didn't work. She couldn't concentrate on the screen. Claudia clasped her hands together, fingers interlaced so hard they ached at the joints. It was almost like a prayer. I hope they catch who did this, for this man's family's sake, if nothing else, she thought. Then she rubbed her hands, palms sliding against each other, trying to forget his icy grip. But it was a hard, cold thing to let go. She couldn't seem to let it go.

3 A COOKIE CUTTER SERMON

Claudia hadn't really planned on going to the dead man's funeral. She hadn't met him alive so it seemed strange to intrude on his death. But she kept walking by that flier every time she left her apartment, and after meeting his mother, her mind changed. Funerals were for the living, not for the dead and she had met his family.

"I don't want to go alone," she told Tom. "Would you come with me?"

"Why do you want to go?" he asked.

"I need some answers," she said.

"But Claudia, a funeral isn't about answers," Tom said. "It's about saying goodbye to someone you knew."

"I met his mom, Tom," she said. "I feel like I have some kind of connection with this guy. It could have been me out there. It could have been you. Why did this happen?"

"I don't know, Claude, but you are traumatized enough," he said. "It seems morbid to go to a funeral of a guy you didn't even know."

"I found him in a snow bank, for Christ's sake," she said. "I found him. It doesn't matter if I knew him or not. I want some kind of closure on this."

"You think you'll get that from a funeral?" he said.

"Fine, we'll go," Tom said. "But I don't think it's good for you, Claude. I think you need to step back from this, try to forget about it."

She clasped her hands together tightly on her lap again and said nothing. He studied the pain on her face with an artist's precision.

"If you really think it will help," he said softly. "Then I'll come with you."

When the two got to the church, the dead man's mother was clutching Alice's arm at the entrance. Alice, their neighbor, was wearing a black blouse with long sleeves and a black skirt that fell just below her knees. Tom stared at her long, sleek calves, while Claudia walked closer to hear the conversation.

"Thanks so much for everything you did for my son," the dead man's mother said, sniffling. "He used to come back from your group repeating the mantra. 'Divine love will set you free.' He was so hopeful for a change. I got a few more years with him, at least."

"I'm sorry I didn't do more," Alice said, her face scrunching up. Her kind, blue eyes brimmed with tears. "Maybe I could have prevented his death. I never should have stopped running that rehab group."

"Oh honey, there's nothing you could've done," his mother said. "He made the choices he did, the bad friends he did."

"Let me know if there's anything I can do for you," Alice said. Her eyes were red and watery. "I know it's a difficult time."

A man took Steve's mother by the arm and walked her shakily down to the front pew. Claudia walked up to her neighbor.

"I didn't know you knew him," she said.

Alice grimaced and nodded her wavy blond hair. "I'm really not supposed to talk about it. Confidentiality. You know I'm a psychologist."

The three of them sat down in the wooden pews and stared

straight ahead at the closed coffin. Alice clutched a little flier close to her chest and inhaled sharply. It had Steve's photo and biography on it. He was born in Missouri.

"Why are you guys here?" Alice asked.

"I found him. I met his... I just want to kn..." Then the blast of organ music began, cutting off all explanations.

Claudia folded her hands in her lap, her fingers locking themselves together again in a type of strange prayer. They seemed to do this whenever she thought of the dead man. The muscles constricted and her fingers went almost bloodless white, trying to squeeze out the muscle memory, the feeling of his dead touch. Tom looked down at her hand and placed his hand on top of hers for a moment. The reassuring warmth of his hand brought Claudia back into the present.

She was listening in and out to the sermon and it struck her how cookie cutter it all seemed. The pastor spoke about death as a transformation, "just like iron rusts and breaks down and then is melted, molded, recast and reborn into something new..."

Claudia couldn't seem to concentrate on the words. She looked around the church at all the people dressed in black sitting on wooden pews. The family shrieked and cried, as expected. Some had the bloodshot eyes of sorrows drowned in alcohol. The sermon didn't fit. It was meant for an old man, not a young one struck down, Claudia thought. The pastor didn't know Steve Jackson well, if he knew him at all.

A few young girls ran about in black dresses, with their dolls. Claudia saw a few faces she recognized. Another neighbor, Sara Johnson, was in the middle of the rows. Her eyes had a glassy look. She was also looking for something in the church. Judging by the way she wrung her hands, she wasn't finding it.

Claudia had to crane her neck to see Stan standing awkwardly in the back of the church in a black suit and tie. The trousers were too long for him and bunched at his ankles and hung over the backs of his shiny black shoes.

After the sermon, people lined up to visit the casket and

milled about. Tom chatted with Alice. Claudia didn't like the way she put her hand on his shoulder and steadied herself against him, so she went over to talk to Stan.

"Do you always come to the funerals of victims?" she asked.

"Sometimes, if the family wants me there," he said. "Steve's mom seems to think I have some special ability to detect the guilty party just by looking at them."

"So she thinks it was someone he knew?"

"Not necessarily," Stan said, shifting on his feet. He crossed his arms and scanned the crowd. His brown eyes were always searching, and worry lines had worn into his forehead, but he was still a good-looking man, albeit a bit worn.

"I can hand out my card, listen if someone wants to talk. Sometimes, it just seems to help, seeing the same people that the victim saw during his life," he said. "It paints a picture, like the grieving widow who's not really grieving. That's not the case here, obviously, but sometimes you can see things. Of course, seeing and knowing is not the same thing as proving."

"Sounds like a hard job," Claudia said.

"People want to pretend the dead guy is an angel, but he was a drug dealer and an addict."

A woman a few feet away turned and glared at him, but Stan's expression didn't change.

"You know what the worst part of it is?" he said. "This kind of crime has a way of spreading like an oil spill. These things tend to escalate. You better keep calling me, honey."

His cell phone started to vibrate. "Excuse me," he said and turned and ducked into the hall.

Claudia noticed Sara Johnson, with her head down, about to leave and touched her arm. Her husband was notably absent.

"So you knew Steve, too?" she asked. Claudia had always been curious to start up a conversation with her, but afraid after all the late-night fights she had overheard between her and her husband. But here was a chance to talk surrounded by civilized people.

"I did." She pushed back a strand of red hair behind her ear.

"I'm sorry for your loss," Claudia said. As she spoke she couldn't help but scan the woman's pale, freckled face for dark bruises. Despite the noises she had heard upstairs, she couldn't find any. "How did you know Steve?"

"He was a friend," she said.

"How did you meet him?" Claudia said.

"None of your business." She inhaled sharply and turned to leave. She kept scratching her freckled arms like she was allergic to her coat.

Tom approached, carrying his jacket and Claudia's. He had a thoughtful look on his face.

"Let me guess," he whispered. "It's confidential."

They walked on crunchy shoveled sidewalks past blocks and blocks of cars until they got to the old, mangled Nissan.

"You know Alice kind of looks like Gwyneth Paltrow when she dresses in black," Claudia said.

"A curvier Gwyneth Paltrow," Tom said. "Maybe." "It almost looked like you were trying to pick her up," Claudia said, scowling.

"What's it to you," he said, with a smirk.

"Well, it's kind of tacky to pick up women at a funeral, don't you think?" she said.

She wasn't sure why it bothered her so much all of a sudden. She'd seen him pick up women before, but at a funeral? Really. That must be why it bothered her.

Claudia pulled shut the delicate, rusted car door a little too hard.

"In any case, I didn't think she was your type," she said. "From what I understand the religious organization she works for is pretty old-school about sex out of wedlock."

"I could still ask her out," he mumbled.

"Maybe she could convert you," Claudia said.

"Or I could convert her." He laughed and gripped the handle above his seat as the car accelerated jerkily through the snow. "Just kidding for Christ's sake!"

Claudia sighed and shifted gears.

"Only you would joke after a funeral," she sighed. But somehow, the distraction made her feel better for a moment. Her hand loosened its iron grip on the gear shifter.

When they got back, they ran across Alice fumbling with her keys outside the front door. Her hands were shaking.

"Are you ok?" Claudia asked.

"Not really," Alice said.

"Would you like to stop by our place for a drink?" Tom asked.

She hesitated for a moment and then said, "Sure."

Claudia was surprised Alice agreed to come over.

Tom couldn't help but raise his eyebrows as he poured out two glasses of bourbon and handed one to Claudia and one to Alice sitting on the couch.

"I may work at a religious nonprofit, but I'm not a saint, you know," Alice said with a sheepish smile that quickly faded.

"Everything's good in moderation," Claudia said, taking a swig and wiping her mouth with her wrist.

"You know, talking is really helpful in situations like this," Alice said. "It's important to create a safe place after a traumatic event, to talk to someone, debrief and decompress."

"I talked with Steve's mom for five minutes and I felt like my heart was going to explode," Claudia said, crossing her arms and gripping her elbows tightly. "So sad. How do you do it? How do you psychologists listen to these terrible stories all day? Don't you get depressed?"

"We've got a lot of training on how to deal with it," she said, "But it's still hard. You can actually get secondhand post-traumatic stress syndrome, if you aren't careful. You can always call me, if you want to. I have a lot of clinical experience with these things. Sometimes it helps to write, pray, meditate, whatever works for you."

Alice's eyes glazed over as she nursed the bourbon and looked off into one of Tom's paintings. It was a small figure at the end of a winding road paved in odd dark purplish bricks. Claudia could never figure out if the black silhouette was skipping or the person was about to fall down, grabbing their leg in agony. She loved the ambiguity in Tom's work. She loved getting lost in his pictures when she didn't want to think about reality and lately she found herself staring at them a lot.

After about three drinks, Alice was sitting on the couch, holding her head in her hands.

"Confidentiality doesn't really matter anymore. He's dead," she sniffled. "I should've never stopped running that rehab group. Healing through faith helps so many people. Why couldn't it work for Steve? I'm sure they found meth in his bloodstream during the autopsy."

Her blue eyes scrunched up and she touched her face with her sleeve.

"Is that how Sara knew Steve? Through the group?" Claudia asked.

Alice nodded. "I knew the two of them kept meeting up on the side. I knew she was married.

"I try not to judge these people," Alice said. "It doesn't really help anything. They already feel bad enough about their own lives."

Tom sat close to her and placed a hand over hers.

"So it isn't a coincidence those two are always fighting and we find a dead guy outside?" Tom mumbled.

"I don't know," she sobbed. "You know, I should never have stopped running that group. I feel responsible. Maybe I could have done something differently. I just keep remembering his face."

She leaned forward on the couch and pressed her hands against her face, wiping away tears.

"Maybe Steve was visiting her and it got ugly with her husband," Tom said,

"Dan Johnson did show up to the meetings once. There was a scene. He said... oh God... I feel like I'm going to be sick," she said.

"I better go. I'm sorry. I don't normally drink," she said, crying and wiping her face on her sleeve. "I should go home. I should go to sleep.

"I just don't know if I can. It's just, the whole thing has me so upset."

"I know, I know." Tom held her shoulders in a light hug as he walked her out the door into the hallway.

"It will be OK," he lied softly. He closed the door and came back to find Claudia on the couch, with her hands clasped tightly together.

"Are you thinking of Steve Jackson," he asked.

"Yes, of course," she said.

"You're holding your hands like that again," he said, gently prying apart her fingers. "You do funny things with your hands when you are thinking of him."

"I just can't seem to get that sensation of his cold fingers out of my head," she said. "It was so cold. Doesn't it bother you?"

"Of course it does," he said. "But I try not to think about it. What can I do about it anyway?"

"Stan said we should keep our eyes and ears open," Claudia said.

"The cops will figure it out soon," Tom said softly, lying for the second time that night. "We don't have to worry about it anymore."

4 MURDER ON THE EARS

Spring came and the radiators turned off. The rickety windows opened, held up by frayed, ragged ropes in the frames. The smell of fresh, wet soil wafted in with the breeze.

The warm spring air brought a talentless street performer to the same corner where Tom and Claudia had spotted the body. Claudia had become compulsive about looking down from the window ever since the body had been found. The fat man clutched his saxophone and spewed out a torrent of senseless notes up and down, unaware of the significance of the brown grass where he stood.

The fluttering "music" continued for hours, days on end, up and down, up and down the scale. From the window, Claudia watched people toss quarters into the saxophone case and growled.

"Don't encourage him," Claudia shouted too quietly for them to actually hear. "I'd like to kill that bastard if he doesn't shut the hell up."

"The man's only trying to make a living," Tom said.

"I guess I can sympathize with that," she said.

She stepped away from the window and sat down. She crossed her legs and it felt like her foot was on fire. It kept bouncing up and down in no particular rhythm, enflamed by the cascade of notes.

The noise seemed to bother the neighbors next door, as well. Claudia wondered what the latest squabble was about. Sara and Dan Johnson just sounded like two mutts in an alley, crashing into pieces of metal, toppling and shattering glass.

She had Stan's cell phone number programmed into her cell. She called him.

"What is it, dear?" he said.

"The Johnsons are fighting again," she said. "One of these days that bastard's gonna kill her."

"I wish she'd press charges," he said. "We'll break it up again. You know, you can always call dispatch."

"But then I wouldn't get to talk to you," she said.

Claudia heard a loud crash.

"Fuck," she said. "I gotta go."

It sounded like the furniture was moving and scraping the wall. She leaned an ear against the wall then backed away.

"What's going on in there?" she said. Tom shrugged.

Five squad cars pulled up silently, with their lights flashing. The saxophonist grabbed his instrument and ran.

A female police officer pulled Dan Johnson out of the front door roughly by the arm. Her ponytail swung back and forth as she jostled him across the sidewalk in handcuffs.

"She's the one who started it," he yelled. "She assaulted me."

"Sure, buddy," she said. "Like I haven't heard that before."

After the cop loaded him into her squad and drove off, Claudia stopped Stan. He had the door to his Ford Crown Victoria open and one foot in.

"Hey, did you ever find the guy that killed Steve Jackson?"

"I help out but I'm not in charge of the investigation," he said. "It's a joint investigation at this point. Even the FBI and DEA have been involved. And no, we haven't caught the killer, yet. Sorry, darling."

"If you guys don't catch him soon, I'm going to start asking my neighbors nosy questions. I think about it all the time."

Stan looked side to side nervously. "Get in the car," he said.

They climbed in and slammed the doors shut.

"You know, I like you, sweetheart. I mean as one friend to another."

Claudia rolled her eyes. She knew she should be annoyed by his terms of endearments. But she couldn't help but like him anyway. Judging by the lines around his eyes, she always got the impression that he cared about what he was doing a little too much.

He started the engine and turned and looked at her.

"You didn't hear it from me, but we think someone in your building killed him," Stan said, hitting the button to roll up his windows "Keep your doors locked, dear. Call us if you hear anything, but don't go getting involved in things that don't concern you. Be careful. This is organized crime we're talking about."

"I'm not scared of gangs," she said to Stan as he drove her back to her corner. The words came out like a lie.

When Tom got home she told him about the conversation.

"I saw Stan," she said. "The cops think it was someone in our building,"

"Christ," Tom said.

"How do we know the police have it right?" he said. "They could be wrong, you know. I hope they're wrong."

She bit her fingernails.

"Who all could it be?" he said. "Let's go down the list of neighbors."

On the first floor, there was Alice and across the hall, there was Janice and her teenage son, Kevin.

On the second floor, Doris, an elderly woman, could be seen clutching the banister on occasion on her way down to get the mail. They occasionally spotted her wearing a robe and slippers. Across the hall lived Mr. Washington, a middle-aged man and his younger wife, Sofia. They hadn't seen Sofia in months.

"It's like she has just disappeared," Tom said.

Claudia and Tom lived on the third floor across from the

constant fighting of the Johnsons, Sara and Daniel. There was also the building manager, Ted, but Claudia wasn't sure if he counted. Claudia realized just how little they knew about the neighbors.

"I'm gonna start asking the neighbors questions." Claudia said. "Let's start with you.

"Tom," she said. "I know this is a stupid question, but is there anything you want to tell me about that night or your past?"

"No, of course not," he said looking her square in the eyes. "Do you have anything you want to tell me?"

"No," she mumbled, her face flushing red.

"You don't suspect me, do you?" he said.

She paused and didn't know what to say.

"Well, goddammit, Claude," he said. "Really? Seriously?"

She sighed. "No, of course not. I really don't. It's just I'm worried."

"Worried about someone killing you in your sleep? I'd be the last person to do that," he said, throwing up his hands. "Besides, if I wanted to, I could have done it a long time ago. Don't you think Stan would have given you a head's up if he thought you were living with a killer?"

"I just want answers," she said loudly.

"You are better off leaving this alone," Tom said. "Don't get involved. If you're worried about it, we should try to move."

"It's not just that I'm worried," she said. "I'm bored out of my fucking mind, and I can't stop picturing that man's face in my head and trying to figure it out. I can't just keep sitting around surfing the Internet trying to find a job, trying not to think about it. Sometimes, I don't even leave the apartment all day. I'm going to talk to the neighbors, even the crazy ones."

"Yeah, let's ask Dan the next time he gets home from jail," Tom said. "What if you get killed? You should just leave it alone. Try to forget about it. It's gang related. It has nothing to do with you."

She crossed her arms and sulked.

"Of course, it has to do with me. I found the guy, dammit."

"I'm just worried about you," he said. "I don't want to see you get hurt."

"I'll be ok. I can take care of myself."

"If you knew what was good for you, you'd leave it the hell alone," he said. "It's crazy to get involved."

She knew he was right. But ever since she was a kid, she had always itched towards recklessness. For Claudia, boredom was hell.

When she was 12, she wanted to bolt after a tornado instead of taking shelter in the basement. She remembered standing stupidly by the window staring at the murky mix of green and black sky when the funnel cloud started to approach. That was before her mom came and dragged her back down to the basement. The woman was always dragging her down, she thought. It wasn't easy growing up as an only child in that house.

"I'm sorry, but I can't just let it go," she said. "At night, I can't help but think over and over, it isn't right what happened to that man. Someone did this to him and they're still out there and I can't fucking sleep."

Claudia wasn't lying. She was averaging four to six hours a night with the nightmares. She just wanted them to stop. She wanted to stop remembering those dead eyes, the frozen skin grazing her fingers.

The killer was still out there, possibly next door. It could happen again. She wondered if she had seen his face, shaken his hand. She wondered which neighbor it was. Was it Dan Johnson? Did Tom have something to do with it? Every night, the fear was like a tornado racing and tearing through her thoughts. She wondered if she had ever seen his face.

"I just want answers," she mumbled. She was going to rule them out, all the neighbors one by one and figure out who did this, if she had to, at least rule them out so she could sleep at night without wondering, constantly wondering. She was going to rule Tom out, too.

5 THE SHUT-IN

Claudia had woken up at 4 a.m. and couldn't fall back asleep. Flopping around in bed like a half dead fish had become a nightly ritual for her ever since the murder. Her mind and body would not sit still. I have to do something, she thought. I can't just lie here. I need answers. I got it, she thought, I'll make cookies, start talking with the easiest neighbors. It seemed like a good idea at the time. She got up, washed her face and stared at the blue circles under her eyes in the mirror. Then she got to work, humming a sugary Julie Andrews song, "Start at the very beginning, a very good place to start." It was a sugary, morbid beginning to an amateur murder investigation, she thought, scolding herself as she laid a dough-covered spoon on the countertop.

Tom stretched his arms up overhead and yawned as he walked into the kitchen. The scent of burnt cookies hung heavy in the air. The counter was littered with flour and broken eggshells. He scratched his hair. It was sticking up in all directions.

"You have no business being in my kitchen." he laughed and waved his hand to dissipate the faint smoky haze.

"Oh, come on. I chose an easy recipe, chocolate chip cookies," Claudia said. "How hard can cookies really be?"

"Um, you did time them, right, Claude?"

"They didn't look done right away," she said defensively.

Claudia bit into a charred cookie with a crunch and tasted black ash. "Ah vel," she said and spat it out into the sink.

"Wow, those look awesome," Tom said sarcastically. "You're such a domestic goddess."

Claudia scrunched up her face and salvaged the least burnt of the cookies, assembled them onto a plate, and covered them with plastic wrap.

"Where you going with those delectable culinary creations?" Tom mocked.

"Downstairs to knock on Doris' door," she said.

"Are you trying to kill the poor woman?" he pointed to the plate and grinned.

"No, I'm just going to ask her some questions. I figure she's the easiest person to start with. She always seems so lonely."

"About the murder? What if she's not home?" he opened up the laptop on the kitchen table.

"That's the nice thing about shut-ins. They're always home," Claudia said as she put on her flip-flops.

Doris peered through the peephole and looked at her. A small ball of fur yip-yapped and slammed against the bottom of the door.

"Hello," she said over the yapping and repeated thumps. "What do you want?"

"I made too big a batch, and I thought maybe you'd like some cookies. Maybe some company too for a minute." Claudia said. She looked away from the hole self-consciously.

It sounded ridiculous when she said it out loud, kind of like something the wolf would say to Little Red Riding Hood's grandmother to get her to open up.

The dog continued to yap. "Shut up, Fifi," the old lady said.

Claudia could hear the clicking of a lock, then another click, and a third click and the sliding of a chain, before Doris turned the knob.

"Come in," she said, her voice shaking slightly.

They walked into her living room. Magazines and papers were piled high next to two old, green and pink floral print sofas. The dog circled dangerously underfoot, threatening to trip its owner.

As Claudia handed Doris the plate of cookies, she noticed the faint blue veins under the wrinkled skin of her pale hands. She must at least be in her late 70s, she thought. All it would take is one trip on the books to snap a hip.

"Doris, you know if you ever need anything, groceries, help around the house, let me know," Claudia said, as she surveyed the clutter and peeling paint on the walls. "It's not like I have anything better to do."

"No, that's not really necessary. I'm sorry. I don't have visitors often," she said, pushing up her glasses. "Please pardon the mess. I like everything within arm's reach, you know. It irritates the bajeezus out of me when people come over and put my stuff away. I can never find it again. Would you like some coffee?"

"Sure," she said. "It might help the cookies go down easier."

"My poor girl, who taught you to bake like this?" she said. After one bite, she squinted hard at the cookie, then put it back down on the plate. "It was a sweet gesture. Thanks."

Doris patted her on the arm, instantly reminding Claudia of her own grandmother who obviously never taught her how to bake cookies.

"So what brings you to my humble abode?" Doris said.

"To tell you the truth, I thought it might be nice to know more about my neighbors after that murder," Claudia said. "It would make me feel safer. Do you know what I mean?"

Her teeth bit into one of her rock-hard cookies and she gulped down the dry crumbs with the coffee.

"Yes, I do," Doris said, offering a lonely, eager smile and leaning forward in her chair. "When I was younger, people used to stop by all the time. Now, everyone is glued to their TVs or their computers, even their phones when they go to the restroom. It's like people have retreated into their own little worlds."

Ironic words for a shut-in, Claudia couldn't help but smile.

"We used to play card games and have dinner at each other's houses," Doris continued. "We'd even spank each other's children. No one locked their doors. Even here. You didn't need to."

"When did that all change?" Claudia asked. The fluff ball growled and chewed on the edge of her pant leg. She couldn't see its eyes.

"I'm not sure." Doris sank back into the flowers of her floral print couch cushions. "It seemed like it happened overnight. I admit I miss the old days, sometimes. My family has all moved away to New York. My daughter works for a bank down there…"

She scooped up the dog and stroked the long, black and white fur on its back. Wispy fur balls collected at the edges of her strokes and fell onto the couch.

"They never visit." She patted the dog on its small head. "I've threatened to leave all my money to Fifi here, but they still never visit."

She put Fifi back on the floor and he started to growl at Claudia again like it was somehow her fault.

"You're retired now?" she said, shaking out her leg, with the tiny dog once again holding onto the edge of her jeans with its miniature fangs. It leaned backward and tugged. Its small nails clack, clacked on the wooden floor.

"Yes. I used to work in retail downtown selling perfume. What do you do?"

"I'm in the process of deciding my next step on the career path," Claudia said with a sigh and an uneasy nod. "I'm kinda lost."

"Laid off?"

"Yep."

"Well, good luck to you." Doris pulled her lips into a sympathetic frown lined by the remnants of bright pink lipstick. "Happens to a lot of people these days."

"Let me know if you hear of any good jobs," Claudia said. "Maybe I'll go back to school if I can decide what I want to do."

Doris gave a sympathetic nod.

Claudia eyed her and quickly crossed her off her list. She was too small and frail. She tried to imagine her wielding a large metal object and attacking a man and envisioned her toppling over and breaking her hip.

"That murder was nasty business, wasn't it?" she said.

Doris nodded. "They never caught the guy, did they? I keep telling the police it was Kevin, but they don't listen."

"Kevin?"

Claudia thought of the tall, lumbering teenage boy with the gut and the dark skin. He was always carrying around bags of fast food, McDonald's, Taco Bell and Burger King. Sometimes, he couldn't wait to get into his mom's apartment, before the bulging cheeks would appear. He was always chewing something and rarely spoke and when he did it was a mumble through mouthfuls.

"Why Kevin?" Claudia asked.

"I know it in my gut that boy is up to something," Doris said, her gray eyebrows furrowing together. "These youngsters today, all rotten. Playing violent videogames, watching nasty videos. You can't trust 'em. Plus, when their kind started moving into the neighborhood, things started to get crazy around here."

"What's that supposed to mean?" Claudia leaned back and the hairs on the back of her neck started to bristle. She took a breath and tried to remember that calling out Doris for being a racist old bat wasn't going to get her any clues. She inhaled uneasily with a loud breath.

"Nothing," Doris said flatly.

"Did you actually hear or see anything that night to make you think it was him?" Claudia said, leaning away in her seat.

"I didn't hear nothing, but that's not saying much. I usually take out my hearing aid at night. It's pretty inconspicuous isn't it," she said, proudly tapping a bulging piece of nude-colored plastic lodged inside her ear.

"Yeah, it is," Claudia said, swallowing. "Well, Doris, I'd better be going."

"Come back anytime," she said eagerly with a big, lonely smile. "Bring your husband, too."

Claudia cringed as she walked out the door with her shoulders up to her ears.

"He's not my husband."

Doris opened her mouth and let out a judgmental "oh."

It reminded Claudia of the argument she kept having on the phone with her mother. "You're living with a man? Why don't you two just get married?"

"Mom, we're not even dating," she would say. "He has a girlfriend."

Well, at least he had a girlfriend before they moved in and he had had a few short-term girls since then, off and on, so it was usually the truth and not a lie.

"I swear there's nothing between us," Claudia told her over and over again. "We are just good friends, roommates, that's all. He's like a brother to me."

If you say something a thousand times, it starts to sink in eventually, right?

Unfortunately, her mother believed the same thing.

"You two should really just get married," she would repeat.

That's when Claudia's voice would start to hit the high notes and Tom would start laughing in the background.

6 A CLOSE STRANGER

Claudia hated being interrogated about Tom. There were just too many questions she didn't know the answer to. She didn't know anything about his childhood. She didn't know anything about where he was from. And she didn't know what he was doing the night Steve Jackson died. Sure, he said he was sleeping, but how could she know for sure?

She scrubbed the dishes from her baking spree with a kind of violence. She scraped steel wool against aluminum with the murky, lukewarm water lapping at her hands.

She never asked him many questions. He had a way of clamming up. He would literally get up and go into his room and lock the door. Sometimes, he'd paint. Sometimes, he'd just stew. Sometimes it had to do with her, but most of the time he just seemed to be stewing in his own bad memories, judging by his scowl.

She never had the heart or guts to ask him again where he was that night, but she always wondered about it. She had gone to bed by 11 that night. He asked her if she had heard anything.

"No," she said. "I'm a deep sleeper."

And that had been the end of the conversation. He never volunteered anything more. It was typical of him to shut up like that when she had a million questions racing through her mind.

Maybe it was time they parted ways. They had started out as temporary roommates and never meant to live together permanently. Maybe it was time to move back in with mom. She shuddered. No, she'd rather die.

Her friends always asked her why she didn't date him. She liked him, but it would have made things too complicated. Claudia had a bad track record when it came to love. She had never been able to be friends with an ex. The good and bad feelings just had a strange way of hanging on forever. She couldn't afford to get confused right now. She couldn't afford to complicate things when she depended on him so much.

He was not bad looking with that strong jaw, those dark eyes, a golden complexion and a daily pushup habit that showed when he was shirtless coming out of the shower. A lot of women liked him, until they realized he was a lost dreamer with very little money. That didn't matter to her.

What did matter was that she had a safe place to stay with a decent roommate. She didn't want to move back in with her mother. Claudia scrubbed the dishes harder just thinking about the prospect. It was always possible, but it wasn't ideal. The bills were piling up. No, she'd go bankrupt before she walked back into that house. Meanwhile, Tom was paying the phone bill and the electricity, while her savings had trickled and dwindled. She bit her lip. She didn't know how she was going to repay him.

Her mother didn't approve of the arrangement, of her living with a man, and wanted her to marry him. But in general, her mom wasn't a good judge of character after two divorces. There was always something off-kilter with Tom, something not quite normal. Sometimes it was a good thing, sometimes not. It was a mix of genius and madness. She started to make a list of the pros and cons in her head as she washed the dirty dishes from her baking spree.

Cons: What kind of grown man honest to God believes in time travel? She wondered.

As her fingers rinsed silverware under the cold water, Claudia thought back in time to when she first picked him up in a club. This was when she actually had a little money and could afford to go out. About a hundred people were gyrating around them, grinding to the pulsing music. Girls flung their hair through the air and shook their booties. Guys did pelvic thrusts and bopped their heads up and down like an army of robotic clones.

All of her girlfriends had already left her, each hand in hand with one of the clones. Claudia was still looking around, waiting for something original. Maybe it was the wrong place to look. A man kept coming up behind her and gyrating against her ass. She had to grab his hands to keep them out from under her shirt. Geezus, she thought. This one's way too wasted.

"I have a boyfriend," she said.

"I won't tell," he said.

It wouldn't have happened if they had followed the golden drinking rule: Leave no girl behind.

Tom stood out in his simplicity and the fact he wasn't trying so hard. He wore a simple white shirt and drank vodka laced with ice cubes. He didn't have gel in his hair. He wasn't trying all that hard to get her attention, but he gave her a soft smile.

She walked over to him at the bar and was relieved when he didn't start incessantly groping her.

After a few drinks together, he asked to come home with her. She said she couldn't. She just wasn't that kind of girl.

"Please, you don't understand. I really don't have anywhere else to go tonight," he said.

Why did she believe him? There was something about him she trusted, a kindness in his eyes. She paused for a moment and drank out of the thin, red straw.

"Fine but no sex," she told him. "I don't take strangers home."

Ultimately, it was the four long islands that made her agree, because taking a stranger into her home was exactly what she was doing. She felt drunkenly invincible.

"That's fine," he said. "I've got a girlfriend anyway."

"Why doesn't she let you stay with her?"

"She's mean," he said, leaning closer to her and touching her arm. "Maybe I should find someone nicer. Someone like you."

"Oh, so original," she laughed, as she tried to hail a cab full of people. She shivered and he put his jacket around her shoulders without asking if she was cold.

Claudia didn't remember exactly what happened after that, but when she woke up the next morning, she had an artist sleeping in her spare room and he hadn't left since. She was almost disappointed he turned out to be such a gentleman. At first she wondered if he was gay.

The stranger was strange. The gentleman was gentle.

The first thing he did when he got up that morning was walk through the whole apartment, running his hands along the bare white walls. His fingers touched all the empty surfaces, searching for something that wasn't there.

"What the hell are you doing?" Claudia asked him. She stared at his hands, then the messy black hair sticking up in all directions and his wrinkled, white shirt. He was too lost in thought to care what he looked like.

"How boring," he said more to himself than to her. "Nothing at all on your walls. How can you live like this?"

"I don't really think about it, I guess," she yawned. "It just doesn't seem that important to have something hanging on the walls."

"Really? If I knew you better, I'd slap you," He held back his hand and grinned. "What you've got on your walls is important. Well, to me, at least, nothing's more important than the art that speaks to your soul. It's who you are."

Claudia rubbed her forehead with the tips of her fingers. Even though she was hung over, she couldn't help but smile.

"That's sweet, but I don't have the money to go off buying art," she said. "You're not insinuating that my soul is cheap and empty, are you?"

"Maybe I could help you," he said.

"Yeah, that's an interesting way to put it," Claudia laughed and nervously folded her bare arms. "Cause I'm the one who needs help."

She felt strangely exposed in her T-shirt and flannel pajama bottoms. She may as well have been wearing a negligee the way he seemed to see through her.

"You've got a spare room," he said. "I could paint you some in exchange for room and board for a month. Please. I really need a place to stay for a little while. The honest to God truth is my girlfriend kicked my ass out cause I didn't have anything to contribute to the rent. I swear."

He stared at the floor and crossed his arms.

"What if I don't like what you paint?" Claudia said.

"I promise you will," he said, looking up at her eyes. "I'll paint you some of my best dreams."

"I should just kick you out right now," she said. "I can just see you on the corner with a cardboard sign that says, 'will paint for food.'"

"But you won't," he said, touching her arm.

"I'm not sure. I barely know you."

"Please, Claudia."

"Maybe if you make me pancakes." Her stomach growled. "I'm hungry. I'm a lousy cook. And don't get any ideas."

"Sure, I'll cook for food." He smiled and then he got to work. He pulled out a heavy griddle and set it on the stovetop.

The next day he returned, juggling a torn duffel bag full of his worldly possessions, a dilapidated easel, a stack of canvases and a smaller bag full of tubes of paint.

"It was a bitch carrying all this on the train," he said, throwing the bags down onto the bed in his new room.

"I told my girlfriend, if she still wants me, I'd move back in after getting a decent-paying job. We'll see."

He didn't look Claudia in the eye when he said this.

She didn't like that. She wondered if he had told her he was moving in with another girl, but didn't ask.

She wondered if he was any good as an artist.

It was strangely exciting to see what he would create. She was tired of living alone, anyway.

But it took him days to get started on his painting. Every morning before she left for work, he was sitting in his boxers eating her Cheerios.

"Can you at least put on pants?" she would ask and he would, for a while.

She'd come back from work and he'd be sitting on the couch watching "Judge Judy," and yelling "not guilty!" at the TV screen.

She started to wonder if it was all a lie, if she was just the world's biggest sucker with a mooch living in her apartment. Maybe his ex had it right and he was just a con artist in search of a sugar mama.

"Why haven't you started painting yet?" It made her mouth feel dry and her stomach twinge nervously every time she asked.

"I'm waiting for the right dream," he'd say.

So after ten days, Claudia decided it was time to evict. Just as she was about to raise her fist and knock on his bedroom door, he opened it.

"I've got something to show you," he said, smiling. He grabbed her wrist and pulled her into the room. And suddenly she could smell the paint fumes emanating from the corner, like the smell of wet soil after a rain.

Tom wore a white shirt, which she found odd for someone surrounded by paint, but not a drop had touched the fabric.

It was a brown-haired woman in a white dress on the beach with her feet just touching the shimmering blue water and a black dog sitting neatly by her side.

"That is a pretty picture," she said. "I like it."

"It's you," he said, nervously, with his fingers in his mouth.

"It's hard to tell with her facing away," Claudia said. "But it can't be me. She's got long hair coiled in an updo, and I have short hair."

"It is you, just not you at this moment," he said, crossing his arms. "She's you at a different time. Your hair won't always be short."

"But I like my hair short," Claudia said, patting the back of it. "And I don't have a dog. Don't get me wrong. I like it."

He frowned.

"I love it. I like the light in the picture," she said. It was drenched in a yellow white glow. "I like the way the sunlight reflects off the water and the sand and her skin. It seems like everything is glowing with happiness."

She smiled. The man was actually talented.

Tom explained the inspiration behind his work, over breakfast a few days later. He was just wearing his boxers, of course. After two weeks, she had given up asking him to put on pants. At least he didn't have a beer belly. In fact, his stomach was closer to a six-pack. She usually tried not to look at it. It was too distracting.

"Pleasant dreams?" he asked, when she sat down and started eating half a bowl of Cheerios. It was the last dusty dredges of the box in her bowl, after he had finished most of the box.

"No dreams that I remember," she said.

"Sad," he said. "I dream all the time. That's how I get the ideas for my paintings.

"I believe we time travel in our dreams," he said. "That's the theme of my work. The images we see aren't just random. They're the future, the past and the present without any context. It might be from our lives, past lives or those of others, people long dead or who haven't even been born yet. Even animals. So it doesn't always make a lot of sense to us."

"What about the crazy dreams?" she asked. "Like where you are banging your high school history teacher and flying across corn fields?"

"Well, not every dream predicts the future, but a certain kind of dream," Tom said.

"But how can you tell the difference?" she said.

"You just can. There's a certain vibe, but it is tricky. You are just seeing one little piece of the picture." He used his fingers to form a frame in front of his eyes. "You might not recognize it until years later."

"That's kind of a neat idea," Claudia said. "But I don't know. You really believe that?"

"I really do," he said, rubbing the side of his face with his hand. She noticed the dark red paint lining his cuticles. It reminded her of blood.

She swallowed the last mouthful of her cereal and ran out the door.

In one way, Tom's ideas made him charming. In another way, it was kind of crazy. Just crazy.

There's no way anything like that could ever be true, she thought.

She shook her head and told herself he was not the man for her. She couldn't help but feel something heavy sinking in her gut when he talked about time travel or clammed up about his past. He never wanted to talk about the past.

Pros: He stood by her when no one else was there. He was probably her best friend.

Cons: She didn't want to mess that up.

The truth was Tom was a gamble she wanted to believe in, but she wasn't much of a gambler.

It would have been easier if they'd started dating back then, Claudia thought. Now, there was so much to lose if things went bad. It wasn't about the apartment. Her overprotective mother would be overjoyed to have her move back home. She'd offered to pay for the flight and the moving truck. It was about going back to a life with plain white walls.

She stared at the paintings. The colors seemed off. Claudia loved the imperfections in his art, like a field of grass with purple blades spotting the landscape. She knew he wasn't perfect, but she didn't care. Maybe it didn't matter that she didn't really know him that well. Maybe all the things he hadn't told her didn't matter. Or maybe they did.

7 NEIGHBORLY VIBES

Claudia knocked on Janice's door the next day. This time, she didn't need to make an excuse. Over the years, they'd swapped Christmas cards, spare keys and glasses of milk.

Kevin undid the chain on the door and peeked out the gap. The teenager was still wearing a ratty T-shirt and pajama bottoms.

"Hi," he said, pausing. "What do you want?"

"Is Janice home?" Claudia said a little too cheerfully.

"She's at work," he mumbled.

"Aren't you supposed to be at school?"

Kevin didn't answer the question. "I'll let her know you stopped by." He coughed theatrically and closed the door.

Claudia could smell cigarette smoke and cats from the hallway. Her heart knocked nervously as she pounded on other doors, but no one else answered.

"Whenever I walk by their door, I always hear the TV blasting, even during the day after Janice has gone to work," Claudia said to Tom over dinner. "Why isn't that boy in school? It seems odd."

"Maybe he's dropped out, gotten in with the wrong crowd, or he's just playing videogames all day," Tom said, sipping up a spoonful of tomato soup.

"You sound just like Doris," she said. "Racist old bat."

"But I'm not," he said, pushing the empty bowl away from him. "I'm more like Kevin. I was a dumb kid once, you know. I fell in with the wrong crowd once."

"Oh really, what did you do?" She raised an eyebrow.

"Not telling," he said. "You know I don't like to talk about it. You'll just have to move on to harassing the next neighbor."

Claudia got an easy excuse to talk with Adam Washington, in the form of stray mail. She had never talked to the man, only knew him as a label on a mailbox in an entryway before this. She had seen him scurrying from his car in the parking lot into his home carrying groceries a few times, but never got a hello out of the tall, gaunt man. Framed by a receding hairline, his long, dark face was always contorted like he'd been sucking on a lemon. He always stared away from anyone that crossed his path.

Claudia was relieved to have an excuse to talk to him. It was hard to start a conversation with someone who avoided any eye contact. It wasn't unusual for the mail to be jumbled up in the building. About half of the letters in her mailbox didn't belong to her. Claudia was constantly reshuffling the letters, putting them on the banister in the hallway or slipping them under the appropriate doors. Once she'd gotten a half-opened paycheck that wasn't even hers.

"You gotta love the Chicago postal service," she mumbled to herself. "Consistently ranked worst in the nation."

Sure, she could slide the letter under his door, but it was from a law office and marked urgent. It would be better to make sure he got it right away. She told herself it was a good reason.

Feeling like some kind of sick stalker, she knocked once in the morning, once in the afternoon and once in the evening, before A. Washington's door finally swung open. Every time she tried, the muscles in her stomach seemed to tighten. She was nervous about going into a strange man's home, especially considering he was a possible murder suspect whose wife they hadn't seen for a while.

With the door open, the smell was overwhelming. She thought Doris' place was bad. But here garbage overflowed from the trashcan in the kitchen to the countertops. Tiny gnats circled overhead. A pot of baked beans boiled on the stovetop. He wore a dirty white T-shirt with armpit and collar stains and a pair of flannel pants. A half-empty bottle of rum sat on his kitchen table.

Still standing in the hallway, she handed him the letter and told him she just got it that morning. Grubby hands quickly shredded open the envelope and wet, brown eyes scanned the words. Then he sat down defeated on a chair.

"Oh God," he said, his shoulders hunching forward in a deep slouch.

Ok, so this was an awkward situation, she thought. But Tom knew where she was, she told herself. Tom knows where I am. I have nothing to fear from this broken man.

"Sorry." He wiped his eyes and then leapt to his feet. "Oh shit."

The beans were burning on the stove and pouring over the metal edges, like a frothy army of bloated ants at some kind of sick picnic. The nutty burnt smoke stung Claudia's nose.

"Now, I don't even have anything for dinner," he said, crying.

When Claudia got back to their apartment, Tom rolled his eyes in the kitchen.

"I can't believe you invited him over for dinner," he said quietly.

"You know, it's been years since anyone came over for dinner." Claudia shrugged and gave him a small smile. "Might be fun. Plus it seems like the civilized thing to do. He's going through some rough times."

"Most civilized people would rather eat at a restaurant," Tom said. He sliced through a head of lettuce with a large knife.

"Not exactly fiscally responsible for the unemployed," Claudia said. "I hate having to order a side salad every time. Even if someone else pays, I feel bad."

It reminded her that it had been a while since she had seen some of them, her old work friends, and she started to slouch.

"It's amazing how some people seem to vanish when you don't have the money to buy a round of drinks," Claudia told him as she pulled dishes out of the cupboard. "I'm glad my artist friend has stood by me, at least. Thank you."

She stopped short of kissing him on the cheek and starting laying out the plates on the table instead.

He raised his eyebrows at her and gave her a pat on the arm. "Failed artist friend."

"Even a failed artist gets some respect." She leaned against the counter next to him and watched the blade dance through the carrots on the black cutting board. "And you're not a failure. You just haven't made it yet. You're a great artist."

"Thanks," he said, with a small smile.

"I miss having a fancy, exciting job title." She sighed. "It kind of screws with your self-identity, not having a job. People ask you all the time, what do you do? Well, I used to be this. I used to be that."

Tom rinsed off a tomato under the faucet. She wondered if he could even hear her over the sound of the water.

"I'm starting to think this building is cursed, maybe that's why I can't find work," she mumbled more to herself than anyone. "I can't even decide what I want to do."

"You'll find a job soon," Tom said. He mixed the ingredients together in a bowl, squeezed in half of a lime and let the salt slide from the palm of his hand onto the vegetables. She liked watching him in the kitchen with his apron on.

"I've lived in a lot of nice places before this, didn't have neighbors with this many problems," Claudia said. "Everyone seemed nice and happy."

"Everyone always seems nice and happy when you don't know their deep dark secrets. Pretty much, everyone has some somewhere."

"Even you?"

"Even me."

"Whatever do you mean by that?" Claudia said, playfully

touching his shoulder. "How come you never want to tell me your secrets?" She pouted.

"I'll tell you later," Tom said. "I need to finish cooking the spaghetti. Your new best friend will be here any minute."

When Mr. Washington came, she was relieved to find he had managed to put on a dress shirt over his dirty T-shirt and wore a pair of decent jeans.

He ate three plates of spaghetti before he started talking. Unlike Tom who twirled his noodles expertly against his spoon, he hacked and slashed them with his fork and knife before shoveling them in. The tomato sauce lined the edges of his lips, giving him a sad, clownish appearance.

"Forgive me, but I haven't eaten this well for a long time," he said. "My wife used to do most of the cooking before she left."

"I'm sorry," Claudia said awkwardly, passing him a piece of butter-drenched un-frozen garlic bread. Her elbow brushed Tom's. "So that's what happened to her. We haven't seen her in a long time."

They sat at a small table in the corner of the kitchen, a place where the heat of the oven mingled with the breeze from the back screen door.

"We were married for ten years, you know. She cleaned out most of my bank account and took off with it. Doesn't look like I'll be seeing any of my money any time soon. She even took the cat."

"How much did she do you for?" Tom said.

Claudia kicked him under the table.

"A lot," Mr. Washington said.

"Maybe she got tired of doing all the cooking," Tom said. "I sometimes get tired of doing all the cooking." He shot Claudia a look.

"Tom," she groaned. "Really. Forgive him. He has a way of sticking his foot in his mouth, if you haven't noticed."

"No, that's all right," Mr. Washington said. "Maybe he's right."

"What do you do for a living?" Claudia said, trying to

change the subject. She crunched into another bite of the garlic bread.

"I'm an engineer. Used to be in the Navy"

"Ahh, that's cool," she said. Claudia couldn't think of anything else to say.

"You?"

"I'm looking for a job at the moment," Claudia said, a bit red-faced in the hot kitchen.

He reminded her of Doris in his loneliness.

She heaped a bit more of the spaghetti onto her plate. The wet noodles slipped to one side of the dish, dangerously close to the edge.

"I think it's more important than ever that we get to know our neighbors these days," she said.

"It was pretty freaky, that murder in the winter, wasn't it?" Mr. Washington said, immediately aware of what she meant.

"Did you guys hear anything?" he said.

"Don't think so," she said. She'd gone over the night again and again in her mind, but she hadn't heard a thing. She had always been a deep sleeper.

"Did you?" Tom asked.

"I heard voices arguing in the stairway before it happened," he said. "I told the cops what I heard, but it didn't seem to help. They didn't do anything about it. Still no arrests."

"What were they arguing about?" she asked.

Mr. Washington paused awkwardly for a moment, his mouth still full after taking a big bite out of his bread.

"He was talking really loud and agitated. He said he couldn't do it anymore. He said it was like God was watching him. He said it wasn't right."

"After a while, they left. I was happy to go to sleep, that the conversation was over. I didn't realize. I didn't know the man was dead. I feel bad. What if I had gone out there or opened my door to see what they were talking about? Would he still be alive?" His voice caught slightly in the middle of the question and his lower lip quivered.

After Mr. Washington left, Tom gave Claudia a hard look.

"That guy was a mess. What are we doing now? Inviting murder suspects to dinner?" He scrubbed the plates so hard the ceramic banged loudly against the metal sink. "He could be a murderer. Maybe he had some beef with Steve we don't know about. Maybe the man was banging his wife or something."

"Tom, really," she said, pursing her lips in an effort to look serious. "That man, a murderer? He seems so helpless."

"We should still check out his story. You trust people too much, Claude. Where's his wife?"

"Oh come on. She's divorcing him. Who else are we gonna start cross examining? Maybe we should check out Doris. She could be a cold-blooded killer beating people senseless with her walker," she said.

Tom sprayed her with the nozzle next to the sink.

She yelped and laughed but felt a little guilty.

"Here we are making light of a tragedy," she said, frowning. "What the hell is wrong with us?"

Tom grabbed her shoulders gently and pulled her toward him in a quick overdramatic hug. "Even when death is outside your door, you still have to live."

Claudia was not quite sure if he meant something more. She looked into his eyes for a minute, then turned away with a small smile. Sometimes, he surprised her. You think you know someone, she thought.

8 KNIVES FLY

Tom and Claudia were eating cereal, and he had just managed to dribble some milk on his work outfit when they heard a loud thud against the wall and a muffled cry for help. It was the Johnsons fighting again.

The two of them sounded like mad dogs in the alley fighting over bones. Claudia had given up trying to figure out what the squabble was about, but it still made her heart pound in her ears every time she heard the yelling and crashing noises.

"Was that the sound of breaking glass?" Claudia asked.

"Yep," Tom said.

"We've got to go over there," Claudia said. "I keep hearing him yelling for help."

"I don't think you should knock on their door right now," Tom said. "Especially when they're in the middle of a fight. You're one crazy woman."

"I'll call the cops first," she said, dialing Stan.

"Call Stan, but really, let's not go there." Tom grabbed her shoulders. "Why do you always have to get all up in everybody's business?"

"That's just the way I am," Claudia said, pushing him away.

Stan told her the cops were on the way. But the muffled cries for help continued.

49

"I can't wait," she said.

She started to walk out the door and Tom followed. The milk had dried to a white crust around his collar.

They walked across the hall and she knocked on the door.

"Are you guys okay?" she yelled. Stupid question, she thought, especially since they could hear muffled cries on the other side of the wall.

To her surprise, Tom reached for the doorknob. Not only did he turn the knob, but the door swung open.

At the same instant, a kitchen knife sliced through the air, brushing the side of Tom's face and embedded itself on the wall behind them. The blade danced against the crumbling plaster.

"Jesus, Tom, why did you open the door?" Claudia shouted.

"He was crying out for help," he said.

For a stunned split second, Claudia peered inside the couple's apartment. It looked like a designer catalog gone mad with a sleek white, leather couch covered in pieces of a broken, green vase. A 50" flat-screen TV hung diagonally on one wall, dangling dangerously. But then they caught sight of Mrs. Johnson with her face puffy and red and framed by red hair flying in wisps.

They retreated across the hall but still witnessed Mr. Johnson flee his apartment in nothing but his boxers, his wife giving chase, this time with a small folding chair. Barely over one hundred pounds, pissed and petite, she had no problem tossing the chair at him as he sprinted down the stairs, with a clunk, clunk crashing sound.

She pawed back sweaty strands of red hair from her glistening face and spat at the floor before huffing back up the stairs.

As Tom and Claudia ran inside their apartment, she yelled, "You bastard!" just as they slammed their door safely shut.

"Yeah, we definitely need to move," Claudia said, panting. "I'm so glad you weren't stabbed to death. Why did you open the door?

"I had to, he was crying out for help," Tom said.

"Do you want to go to the ER?" she asked, cringing as the towel became splotchy red and pink. "Maybe you need stitches."

"I'm ok," he said, looking into her eyes.

She put her hand behind his neck and hugged him for a moment. Blood dripped from a thin line across his cheek. Claudia pressed a warm soapy white towel against the wound.

"It's not that deep," he said, looking into the mirror on the closet door. "Shit, it looks like I've been in a swordfight."

Stan knocked on the door and told them they'd already arrested Mrs. Johnson. Claudia could see a few more patrols out of their window, driving around and still looking for Mr. Johnson. They could even hear the squeal of brakes at the stop signs as the cop cars looped back.

"I won't be able to ask them any questions, I guess," Claudia muttered to Tom. "Not like I would have had the courage to anyway. They were too crazy to talk to."

Tom told Stan that he'd be more than happy to press charges over the knife.

"That bitch nearly did me in," he said, pacing back and forth. "If I hadn't jerked to the right..."

Stan shook his head. "You should have waited for us to get here," he said.

"That dude would have been dead if we hadn't opened that door just then. I've never seen anything like that. You should have seen that crazy bitch."

"Tom, watch the language with the cops," Claudia said.

"How else would you describe her? Please! She was a crazy bitch."

"Ok, fine, I agree," she said, "I'm sorry. I'm being ridiculous, aren't I? I almost got you killed."

Claudia stroked his arm, trying to calm him.

"Why haven't you guys already locked her up?" she turned and asked Stan.

"Well, my dear, they always decline to press charges," Stan said. "The two of 'em always end up at the court house and the judge always asks 'em, 'Sir, are you afraid of her?' and he always says no.'" And the judge asks her, "Ma'am, are you afraid of him?' and she always says no. And the two of 'em walk outta there down the aisle between the rows of seats, holding hands like a pair of goddamn newlyweds."

"This time is different because she tried to impale Tom," Claudia said. "Right?"

"Definitely," Stan said.

"Do you think either of them were responsible for the murder in January?" she asked Stan. "She did have that glimmer in her eye. She looked like she could've killed Tom."

He bit his lower lip and shook his head. "I'm not in charge of that investigation. I only assist.

"But have you ever seen them with the victim or know what reason they might have had for attacking him?" Stan asked.

"No," Claudia said. "But Sara was at Steve Jackson's funeral, so she knew him."

"One other thing," Stan said. "You ever meet a guy who goes by the name Angel?"

Tom and Claudia shook their heads.

"Hispanic male in his late 20s?"

"Who is he?" Claudia asked.

"A person of interest. Well, let me know if you hear anything," Stan said. "But don't do anything stupid. The community is our eyes and ears, but we don't want you gettin' stabbed in the eye." He winked at Tom, and Tom crossed his arms.

Claudia followed Stan as he walked out to his car.

"Out of curiosity, who in my building has a criminal record?" she asked.

"Baby, you live in this city long enough you're bound to know somebody who's gotten into some kinda trouble," Stan said, stepping into his squad and turning on the ignition. "Even your Tom's got a record."

"What do you mean my Tom has a record?" she asked.

"You mean you didn't know? Why don't you ask him?"

Stan laughed. "But keep this in mind, just 'cause someone's got a record, don't mean they're a murderer."

Claudia slammed the front door a little harder than she had meant to on her way back into the apartment. A stream of obscenities spilt out of her mouth as she walked back up the stairs.

But she didn't ask Tom about his record right away when she got back into the living room. The thought made her nervous. She was going to ask him any minute. She knew she should just put it out there but here was the thing. He was still paying her goddamn rent. What difference did it really make? It must have been something small, insignificant. She would ask him later. It would be easier later after she had figured out how to ask, thought about the right words to use, right?

9 CLOSED DOORS

Claudia could feel the icy cold fingers. She could feel the ice-cold skin. She could see his dark and frosted eyes.

She woke up gasping. The thoughts were whirling through her head. The dead man's frozen eyes had burned into her dreams.

She tried to squeeze them out by closing her eyes as tightly as she could. A few tears came out. She flipped onto her stomach and cradled the pillow in one arm, pulling it toward her damp face. Her mouth tasted dry and cottony. She got up for another glass of water. The bed groaned when she left it and groaned when she came back. The springs were shot.

She wondered if she should knock on Tom's door, like a child seeking comfort from a nightmare. But that didn't seem like a good idea. She was scared of his criminal record. She wanted to know, but she didn't want to know. She wanted to ask but she didn't want to ask. Would she think less of him? Would it matter? Why bother asking? After all, he was the one paying the rent lately and he was a good roommate. Would it really change anything?

She needed a job so bad. She wouldn't need him so badly if she had a job. But she knew that was a lie too. She needed Tom for one hundred reasons. She had one hundred reasons not to sleep, didn't she? She had one hundred reasons to toss and turn.

Claudia couldn't fall back asleep, so she just lay there, like a corpse with her hands folded on her belly clasped in an unuttered prayer. She breathed deeply and rhythmically. But the sleep wouldn't come.

She should just get it over with and ask him again. But the thought made her heart pound. The few times she had started to ask, her hands started to shake involuntarily. That's how nervous she had gotten around him lately. It was silly. Here she was, a grown woman with a close male roommate and they had built their whole home life together around not talking about anything serious, avoiding all their real problems.

She got up, tied the string on her pajama pants and walked around the living room looking at his pictures. She couldn't imagine going back to empty, white walls. She loved the paintings.

One of her favorite pictures was propped up on the wooden bookshelf. It was of a little girl walking down a lane full of sunflowers. They were taller than she was. Maybe it wasn't a little girl, but a young woman. It was hard to tell. She was dwarfed by the flowers and her hair hung in braids. Claudia liked the picture because the scale was all Alice in Wonderland. She stared and stared at the image and then went back to bed.

She fell asleep thinking of giant sunflowers and walking down the winding path into a distant, lush, green forest. Then, she started to dream about them swaying in the breeze, snapping a tall stem and carrying the flower like a parasol under the sun. Tom was suddenly carrying his own parasol and twirling it around. "Art can heal," he said.

"You always say dreams mean something," she said. "What does this one mean?"

"I don't know, Claude, you tell me." He leaned over and kissed her. She woke up gasping with thoughts whirling in her head again. What had he done and would it make a difference, she wondered.

She ran through the list of possible offenses in her head. She could forgive shop lifting but not drunk driving, she thought. Smoking a joint was not the end of the world but felony drug possession was not OK. What was she even thinking? She thought. There was no way Tom could have done hard drugs and still have his brains. Well, maybe shoplifting, she decided. She could see him stealing art supplies. Canvases are expensive. He told her so all the time.

It was the same endless loop of worry playing like a bad recording. Who killed Steve Jackson? What was Tom's real past?

For a moment, she lay in her bed, listening to the sounds of the birds and the rain. A sea gull squawked over the whoosh of cars slicing through the water and the low rumble roar of engines.

The new spring leaves outside the window were bright, freshly washed green. Even the building across the street seemed cleaner. The black blemishes of pollution seemed to shrink against the old brick and stones.

She stumbled out of bed and saw Tom sitting on the couch in his boxers.

"How'd you sleep?" he asked.

"Like shit," she scratched her head under the tangled misshapen mess of hair. "I need to stop thinking about this murder."

"Sometimes there is such a thing as knowing too much about people," he said.

"I know," she said.

"You've got one of those faces," Tom said, touching her cheek. "People think they can trust you and you care. With a face like yours, it seems so easy to spill secrets."

"I know what you mean. People are always telling me crazy shit about themselves," she said. "Except you."

"What do you mean?" he asked.

"Tom, do you have a criminal record?"

"No," he said quickly. "Of course not."

She sighed. "Then why did Detective Stan tell me you did."

"It was stupid, juvenile shit, Claude," he said. "It shouldn't count."

"Great, so you just lied to me then," she said. "Why didn't you ever tell me about it? What the hell?"

"It doesn't matter, Claude. I'm a reformed man."

She snickered. "Is there such a thing?"

"I knew you wouldn't understand," he said. "Why do you have to be such a bitch about it?"

"Fuck you, Tom," she said. "I have a right to know these things."

"Look, I'm sorry." His voice was suddenly soft as satin and silk. "You want me to move out, I'll move out. But I'm done talking about this. You have to believe me, it was stupid, juvenile shit." He got up, walked into his room and closed the door.

"Is the truth really so terrible?" she called after him. "Fucking A. Coward. Just tell me what's going on." But the door stayed closed.

What if Tom actually had something to do with the murder? She wondered, grinding her teeth. What if the killer lived in her apartment and not outside of it? It was a sad, paranoid thought. She tried to dismiss it, but it was there in the back of her head as loud as the lie he had spoken.

10 JUVENILE TROUBLE

Claudia was still sitting at home the next day. Although she had sent out a couple of resumes and had a couple of interviews, the only thing she had to show for it was a recently dry-cleaned shirt and a freshly polished pair of shoes waiting in the closet. She searched the job sites for hours, trying not to think about Tom's past or the murder. If she had a job, it would be easier to walk away, if she had to. Did she even want to?

She stared at a freshly painted piece of Tom's artwork, standing on the easel. She loved the smell of paint.

He had the talent but not the ego to make a career out of it. He was never much for selling his work, just happy to churn out painting after painting and stack them in odd places around the apartment, behind the couch, leaned up against the entertainment center, gathering dust in the closet. More than a dozen hung on bathroom walls alone. With the lack of wall space, they were beyond caring about the moisture anymore. Tom liked to say that soap scum and fogged frames were part of his artistic statement.

Even though it was getting crowded, the pictures seemed like old friends. Claudia loved to walk around and visit with them throughout the apartment.

Tom fiddled with his keys at the back porch door and caught her staring at the latest addition through the glass. It brought a smile to his face.

Once, she asked Tom if he ever thought of giving it up and he said he couldn't. "A painter is someone who paints," he said, "And if they don't paint, the paint just starts to ooze out of their pores."

It almost seemed like that's what happened with his latest painting. Red paint had oozed all over the canvas in violent bloody streaks. Tom had painted a picture of pain. Claudia felt a twinge of guilt when she looked at it, like it was her fault he felt that way. He could only paint what he felt, he had once told her.

"It's too bad I didn't get stabbed," Tom said, with a sarcastic smile while he was taking off his muddy shoes. "Then maybe you'd be able to sell some of my work."

"I could use the money," she laughed.

They were both pretending like nothing had happened and it seemed to be working for now. It was an uneasy truce.

Claudia sighed, thinking of her job search. After sitting at home all day, the words were bottled up inside her just waiting to spill out in a long-winded, breathless tirade. He was still her friend, after all.

"Sometimes, I just wish I'd get a goddamn e-mail telling me the position has already been filled but thanks for your interest," she ranted nervously. "Basic courtesy. You shoot off your resume into the online abyss and hope they acknowledge you're a human being, but everything is automated now and that's not how things work anymore. Silence. An e-mail inbox you compulsively check 34 times a day, filled with hundreds of messages from stupid websites that force you to sign up and then send you a constant stream of spam."

She threw up her hands and sighed.

"I'm sorry, Claudia." He said, patting her arm awkwardly. "I'm sure you'll hear back from someone soon."

It was enough to drive her crazy, so she went outside and sat in a plastic patio chair not too far the dumpsters and read one of her neighbor's abandoned newspapers. It had been sitting in its wet orange bag on the ground for three days. She listened to the sounds of birds chirping and squeaky car brakes on the street.

She spotted Janice taking out an oozing bag of trash. Her biceps bulged as she carried it down the wooden stairs, plodding down with heavy, angry footsteps. Her black hair was straightened smooth and pulled back in a stiff ponytail.

Her heavy eyebrows pushed down over her squinted brown eyes. Janice mustered a small, halfhearted smile at the sight of her neighbor, but the angry eyes didn't change.

"Hi, Claude."

"How are you doing?" Claudia asked her.

"You don't want to know," she huffed.

Janice dropped her bag of garbage with a thud into the dumpster and let the plastic lid drop with a bang.

Claudia told herself not to ask her again. It was none of her business, she thought. But somehow the silence was welcoming. Sometimes, silence is ripe for confessions, after all.

"Kevin is being expelled," Janice said, as she lumbered back toward the stairs. "It wasn't his fault, damn it."

She paused by Claudia's chair.

"Wow, I'm sorry to hear that. That sucks."

Janice's upper lip quivered for a moment. "They say they found a gun on him at school," she said through gritted teeth. "But I know that ain't the truth."

"I know a good lawyer if you want the number," Claudia blurted out, unsure of what to say.

She looked it up in her cell phone. Janice ducked inside her unit and came out with torn-off piece of an envelope. She shook the pen repeatedly before scratching the digits onto the paper against the wall.

"I can't really afford this," she said.

When Tom came home, Claudia told him about the conversation, while the two of them sat on opposite sides of the couch.

"That's an interesting tidbit," he said, fingering the TV

remote. "That Kevin must be into all sorts of trouble. Has he gone from bludgeoning people to wielding a handgun now? Or is it just a coincidence that he's started bringing a handgun to school?"

"I still don't think it was him," Claudia said. "Maybe there's a logical explanation for it? Maybe he was set up like his mom said? Maybe it was another kid's gun?"

"Sure, whatever," Tom said. "Like that's likely."

"You really shouldn't stereotype people, Tom," she said. "Didn't we learn anything from Mrs. Johnson? We always thought it was Dan throwing the punches."

"Maybe it was Janice then who killed the guy. It was Kevin's mom then and the apple doesn't fall far from the tree," Tom said.

"Maybe it was Mr. Washington," she said. "Maybe he finally lost it and his wife was having an affair with Steve Jackson."

"Or maybe it was Alice," he said. "And she's got some kind of cult going on."

"Please, how much speculation and bullshit can we come up with?"

"The thing is any one of us could have done it," he said. "If the police don't know, we'll never know, so we just need to forget it."

He turned on the TV and took a bite of his Lucky Charms cereal. A small bit of blue milk dribbled from his spoon onto his chest. He wiped it off with his thumb and continued watching the program, transfixed by CSI Miami.

11 A FEAR OF GOD

Whenever anyone knocked on her door with a handful of pamphlets, Claudia had a tendency to hide as low as she could, far away from any windows. Luckily on the third floor, it had been a few years. But this time, she opened the door, because it was Alice standing there on the other side of the peephole.

Claudia was still afraid she would hand her one of her religious pamphlets and try to convert her. She was afraid Alice would ask her if she was a sinner, if she had accepted Jesus into her heart. All those terrifying questions that people from religious foundations like to ask before telling her she was doomed to burn in hell forever.

Alice wore a sleek form-fitting sweater and pencil skirt with black boots up to her knees. Claudia had heard her clip clop up the stairs.

She slid open the chain and spotted Alice's blue eyes and soft smile in the cracked open door.

"Sorry to bother you," Alice said. "I just wanted to tell you about our fundraising drive and pass on some new brochures. Don't feel like you have to give anything. I'm just kind of excited."

Claudia led her into the kitchen where she already had a pomegranate sliced in half. She cut it into quarters with a long thin knife and the red juices squirted out, splattering the counter and her hands. It reminded Claudia of a medieval bloodletting with the red liquid pooling at the bottom of a bowl.

"Would you like some?" she asked. The white cabinet made a sticky noise as she swung it open and pulled out a bowl.

"I love pomegranates," Claudia said. "There's something so relaxing about peeling one. It's almost like meditation. Do you ever meditate?"

"I do yoga," she said. "Afterward, I'm so relaxed I sometimes forget to look before crossing the street. One of these days, I'm going to get clobbered. I swear it's better than drugs. You get such a nice high from a good exercise session."

How would she know, Claudia wondered.

"So how is work going?" Claudia asked.

Alice was the director of a nonprofit, a religious foundation, in addition to being a psychologist. She was one of those people that made Claudia feel like she was wasting her life.

"Good," Alice said. "Check out the new brochures. I'm so excited."

Claudia repressed a groan and felt her shoulders tighten. Alice handed her a pamphlet. It was glossy and crisply folded.

"Hey, I know that church," she said, looking at the photo. "It's been vacant and in disrepair for years."

"We are going to restore it," she said, "But it's gonna cost a lot, hundreds of thousands, so it's gonna take years before we can hold services there."

"It's a beautiful building," Claudia said looking down at the photos of the grand, old building. "Too bad I don't have any money to donate."

"That's OK," Alice said. "You can volunteer, if you feel like it. It's hard preserving something so historic, keeping it the same, while updating it for modern times. We wanna start a school, too. There was no such thing as handicapped accessibility or fire code back in 1895. Do you have any idea what sprinklers cost?"

Claudia shook her head.

"It's pretty ambitious, I know, but we feel it's important not just for the congregation but the community." Alice wound her long, blond hair around a finger.

"What does it look like on the inside?" Claudia asked. She had always wondered while walking by the giant wooden door and ivy-covered stone walls.

"Once you get beneath the layer of pigeon droppings and graffiti, there is some amazing religious art," she said. "Paintings of Mary and Jesus and all the saints. You should see the colored glass in the dome. It's broken in spots but gorgeous when the sunlight comes through."

"I'd like to see that," Claudia said. She leaned against the kitchen counter.

"When we first started, we used to hold impromptu services in the courtyard, but the contractors won't let us anymore because of all the asbestos and lead paint floating around," she said.

"Where are you working these days?" Alice asked.

"Nowhere," Claudia said, sighing. "I'm still looking for a job."

"Really," Alice said, eyeing her. "Maybe I'll be able to hook you up with one eventually, if things take off."

"The worst thing is not having health insurance," she said.

"What a world we live in." Alice patted her on the shoulder. "It seems like everyone's looking for work, and crime's on the rise."

"I'm still pissed they haven't caught that murderer," Claudia said.

"Yeah," Alice said.

"Pretty terrible to have that happen right below your window," Claudia said.

"It was," she said. "I still pray for that man's family. I knew him. I still can't believe it."

"Did you hear or see anything?" Claudia asked.

"No, I was sound asleep," she said. "You?"

"We didn't hear anything, but the next day we spotted him

from our window," Claudia said. "Really creeped me out."

"I don't think the police are doing a very good job on the investigation," Alice said, sitting back. "They barely asked me any questions at all. I think my whole interview with them took about five minutes."

"What was Steve doing here?" Claudia said.

"I don't know," Alice said. "All I know is he didn't come to see me."

"Was he here to see Sara Johnson?"

"I shouldn't talk about that," Alice said. "You know I said too much already after the funeral."

"He was a dealer. Maybe he had a customer in the building…"

"Maybe," Alice said.

"Sara was in your rehab group too. Does she still have a drug problem?" Claudia asked. "Do you think he was bringing her drugs?"

Alice shrugged and looked away, blinking back tears. "I really shouldn't talk about it, and I really don't know."

Claudia wondered if Alice had forgotten their whole conversation the day of the funeral. Dead men don't need their privacy anymore.

"What kind of drugs was Steve into?"

"Meth," Alice said. "I really shouldn't say anything else."

There was an awkward silence.

"It bothers me too, not knowing for sure what happened," Alice said finally.

Claudia poured herself a glass of water. "The whole thing makes you kind of value your own life a little more, don't you think?" she said.

"Yeah, it does." Alice nodded. "We never know how much time we have left. That's why faith's so important.

"I know you're having a rough time," she said. "If you'd like, maybe we could attend church together, sometime."

Claudia looked into her warm, blue eyes and wondered what to say.

"You know, Alice," Claudia said. "I appreciate your

concern, I really do. But let me find God on my own."

"You're in my prayers," Alice said. "I'm just trying to help."

Claudia gritted her teeth and stared down at the glossy brochures on her kitchen table. She hated pity.

12 MURDER ON THE MIND

Claudia finally got a call from a potential employer while sitting in her bathrobe watching a daytime talk show about different size booties and whether or not they belonged to a man or a woman based on the shadow behind the screen. It was absolutely riveting television. It took her a good five minutes to find her cell phone under the stacks of half-opened bills on the coffee table. The pages flew off the table, fluttering to the ground.

She listened to the voicemail and called back immediately trying to sound casual, not desperate. She'd make a great office assistant, she thought, as she stared at the chaos in the apartment with papers, mail and laundry strewn all over.

She busted out the interview clothes and the high-heeled shoes. She was out of practice so she wobbled in them a bit or maybe they were always a little too big. Her heels slipped out of the edges as she hopped on the bus going downtown.

She called Tom immediately with the news about the interview. He wished her luck.

"Hope this will finally get your mind off our murder mystery," he said. "It's time to move on and let the police worry about it."

Yes, maybe it's time to move on, Claudia thought sadly. If

she had a job, maybe she and Tom could have that conversation.

She stared up at the 50-story black building with its rows of windows after windows. It was an older high rise, a big black box. She had to sort through 50 buttons in the elevator to find the right floor. Her pointer finger danced around and hunted for that button, especially since she was nervous.

Claudia scribbled her name on a visitor's pass, spent five minutes waiting in a gray, drab lobby and found herself sitting across from a middle-aged Mr. Zaleski. She got the impression he was clever. Maybe it was just his old-fashioned, round spectacles. Or maybe it was just the glint in his eye.

"Pardon me," he said, while wiping his nose. "I seem to be coming down wid a cold."

Great, she thought, looking down at her fingers, I just shook your hand.

"So why do you want to work at Rabid Consulting?" he asked.

"Excuse me?" she said. "Oh, why do I want to work at Rabbit Consulting? Because it seems like a great company."

The fact of the matter is she had no idea. Because they pay $17 an hour, that's why, she thought. In reality, she had no idea what Rabbit Consulting did even after visiting their office. Their website simply said they offered solutions to clients. What the heck does that mean? Claudia was tempted to ask Mr. Zaleski but didn't want to blow it.

But as he started talking about his company, she started to tune out.

Maybe her problem was that she kept applying for boring cubicle work, she thought. Looking over Mr. Zaleski's shoulder, she wondered if she really wanted to work in a plastic cave drenched in florescent light, shuffling papers from point A to point B, making copies of meaningless papers and filing files.

Claudia couldn't help but think she'd like to find a job where she made something, did something, created something – tangible evidence of working on something that actually existed, a product. Even if it was working in a sock factory, she thought.

Mr. Zaleski, I would rather make socks than work in this office, she thought.

Instead of telling this to Mr. Zaleski, she gave him her speech about people skills and being a team player.

Claudia gasped when a man suddenly appeared, dangling from a rope outside the window behind Mr. Zaleski. She found it hard to concentrate as the man attacked the window with a suction cup in one hand and a washcloth in the other. He wiped in circular motions and pushed off the glass, flying backward on the ropes. Now, there's a job she'd like, she thought, a window washer.

Mr. Zaleski did not mistake her fascination for window washing as a fascination for filing.

"We have a few other candidates we still have to interview. We'll let you know."

She thanked him, shook his hand and left. She wondered if he would ever actually call.

She wondered if she would like it, working in that office, with her fingers dancing over manila envelopes in alphabetical order, half-time. It was the kind of work was that took hours, but not brains.

As she rode the bus home and stared at the lake, Claudia couldn't help but think about her neighbors. Who was the murderer?

She ran through the list over and over. Doris, Mr. Washington, Alice, Mr. and Mrs. Johnson, Kevin, Ted and finally Tom, but that seemed foolish. What if it were Tom? No. She couldn't even think that's a possibility, could she?

But how would she even know he was in his room that night? He always kept the door locked. It's not like she would know if he had snuck out. And what was the story behind his record and why wouldn't he just tell her?

When she got home, she stared at his latest painting hung to dry in the living room. She stared at its streaks of red paint, smudged black edges, slashes and slashes and the dark outline of a figure beneath. It was the work of a frustrated and ignored artist, one who has given up his dream of sharing with the world.

Poor Tom, she thought. But he's not a murderer even if he does have murder on his mind and a record he's not talking about.

13 A LOCKED DOOR

"I'm taking you out for dinner." Tom pulled a black T-shirt down over his head. "I know you feel like shit not getting that job. The least I can do is take you out."

"You don't have to do that, Tom," Claudia said.

"No, I insist," he said, grabbing her wrist and pulling her off the couch. "You seem down lately. Let's go out."

Claudia didn't have a lot of money. Neither did Tom with his barely over minimum wage job. She knew that.

Sure, the city was full of fine dining establishments, brimming with white tablecloths and chefs with world-famous egos. They could get a 24-course meal for $225 per person, but that was not where they were headed.

They got into her car, an old Nissan with the bumper just hanging on. At high speeds, the rusted hood had a tendency to float upward like an airplane wing.

Tom held onto the handle above the passenger side seat.

"Are you afraid of my driving, honey?" she said.

"No," he said, clutching the handle tighter. "I'm afraid of your car exploding."

"Well, then what's the point of holding onto the handle, then?" she said, smiling and shifting into reverse. "If you are afraid, get your own damn car."

They drove two miles on city streets to their favorite dive Chinese restaurant with its fluorescent sign and paper tablecloths.

They dined on chop suey while admiring the fake red carnations and frayed, faded plastic leaves.

"There is something satisfying about eating food that's cheaper than you can cook it for," Tom said, tapping the wooden tips of his chopsticks together on the plate. "Tasty too."

She rolled her eyes. "One day," she said. "When you make it big, we'll be eating foie gras and drinking expensive wine with your supermodel girlfriend."

"That sounds like a nice threesome. But for now, we don't have to feel guilty about torturing ducks, geese, whatever," Tom said, with a grin. "It's not always about money, you know. There are more important things, like love and enjoying life."

"How romantic," Claudia said, laughing. "Who are you? You're not going to propose here are you?"

"Not here," he said, laughing back.

"Damn," she said. "I could've really used the health insurance benefits.

"Seriously, though, thanks for taking me out," Claudia said. "I'm sorry if I've been a bit of a droopy roommate lately and obsessive compulsive about this murder."

"No apologies needed," Tom said. "It's not your fault I was almost stabbed."

"Yes, it was," she said. "I feel really bad I haven't been able to pay you back for all the rent, too."

"Yeah, I guess it kind of was your fault we were there, but I can think of a few ways you can pay me back," Tom said, raising his eyebrows. "Just kidding."

"You know, Doris thinks you're my husband," Claudia said. "Kind of funny, huh?"

Tom smiled unsteadily as he laughed.

"Maybe we should get going then, my dear wife," he said, taking a long swig of the last of his beer. "What? Just trying it out."

As they got back in the car, Tom tapped his fingers on his leg. Shadows jumped across his face as the car drove between the streetlights.

At home, Claudia flicked on the lights and drew the curtains.

"You know, there are some things I've been meaning to ask you," she said.

"Does it involve a threesome with you, me and Halle Berry?" he said, yawning and sitting down with his arms up on the back of the couch.

"No, I know it's not a big deal but you do have a criminal record." Claudia plopped down next to him and turned her body towards his. "What's it from?"

"Seriously, that's what you're going to ask me right now?" Tom said, pulling his arms crossed close to his body. "That effing cop tells you some trumped up bullshit about me, and that's what you ask me? Next thing I know you're going to ask me if I killed the guy outside in the snow bank, aren't you? Christ."

He stood up and paced across the room. The floorboards creaked at all the usual places.

"Tom, don't you think I have a right to ask simple questions? We live together, after all."

"Don't you know me at all?" It was like he was holding something invisible in his claw-like fingers and shaking it in front of his face. "No, of course, you don't."

"Tom..." she started to say before he interrupted.

"You're frickin' blind." The arm flew down to his side in exasperation. "How many times have I told you, I love the light in this place. You don't get it, do you? Maybe I should move out. You're always going to suspect me of something."

She opened her mouth and closed it a few times. Well, at least she had asked.

"Don't. I just wanted to know for sure..." she said. "I'm sorry."

"Stop playing with me." He slammed his door and locked it behind him. "And don't ask me again."

14 MISSING

Claudia was still in her pajamas when someone banged on her front door.

She ran quietly shuffling her feet to check out who was behind the keyhole and saw Janice's face distorted behind the glass. She opened up.

"Kevin's gone," Janice said. "Have you seen him?"

"No, I haven't, I'm afraid," she said, pushing unbrushed hair behind her ears. "What happened?"

"His expulsion hearing is set for today, but he ain't in his room," Janice said. "He ain't nowhere. He ain't answering his phone. It's been two days."

"Did you call the police?" Claudia asked.

"Yes," she said. "But I don't think they believe me. They think he's just a teenager off partying with his friends. They made me come in and file a report. I had to take a taxi to get to the station. What good does a report do? It's just a piece of paper."

"What time is the hearing set for?" Claudia asked.

"One o'clock," she said, starting to choke on tears. "I can't even get there. He took the car."

"Janice, I'd like to help but can you give me a few minutes?" Claudia said. "I'll be right over."

74

She went back inside her apartment. Tom looked up at her from his perch on the couch. He was eating a bowl of Lucky Charms and drinking the last of the blue milk one spoon at a time.

"After that crazy business next door, why are you getting involved in other people's problems?" he asked.

"The fact of the matter is I don't have anything else to do today anyway," she said. "And how can you turn down a crying neighbor? I think I'd go straight to hell."

Tom stood in the doorway as Claudia brushed her teeth, scraped deodorant under her armpits and applied a little mascara to her lashes.

"Why am I always the depository for other people's problems? Maybe I just know weird people," she said, blinking her eyes. "Maybe I attract them somehow."

"Maybe you just like weird people. Besides, everyone has deep dark secrets," Tom said, leaning against the old white wallpaper. "It's not that people are weird, you just get to know weird things about them after a while. There's no such thing as normal."

Claudia ran the red lipstick around the edges of her mouth, then smacked her lips together.

"I can see why people tell you things," he said. "You seem like you are good at keeping your mouth shut," Tom said, watching as she blotted her full lips with a tissue. "Most of the time."

"You know, I tell you everything," she said. "I'm not great at keeping secrets."

"Well, maybe you're just nosy then," he said. "Good thing I haven't told you mine."

She went into her bedroom, closed the door and picked out some black pants and a crumpled button-up shirt that had fallen off the hanger. Claudia checked her reflection in the mirror, particularly her butt. She would have looked almost professional if it weren't for the wrinkles. But she refused to iron when she wasn't getting paid.

At Janice's apartment, Claudia sank into an oversized sofa

and stared at the clock on her DVD player. It was 10:33 a.m.

"Don't worry about getting to the hearing," Claudia told her. "I'll drive you, if you want me to."

"I'm not sure how much good it will do," Janice said. "If he's not there."

"When did he leave?" Claudia asked.

"Night before last," she said. "We had a fight. He wouldn't tell me about the gun, said he wasn't a snitch. I called him a coward."

"Do you know if he took anything with him? Clothes, money?"

"I hope he has his medication." Janice's forehead was lined with deep grooves of worry.

"Why don't we take a look?" Claudia said.

They opened the door to his room. Claudia was surprised by what she saw.

She always pictured Kevin as the stereotypical messy teenager but there was no chaos. No dirty clothes were piled on the floor. Geometry and chemistry books were stacked neatly on a desk corner. A red electric guitar leaned silently against the wall.

"I didn't know he's a musician," Claudia said. "Is he any good?"

"I couldn't tell you," Janice said. "He always practices with his headphones plugged in, so I can't hear any thing when his fingers dance over the wires. It looks kinda funny when he plays and there ain't no sound. Just metal strings twanging quietly."

"He writes a lot too, I see." Claudia flipped through the notebooks stacked a foot high on his desk. "I didn't have him pegged as a poet."

"Song lyrics," Janice said.

"He didn't have a journal did he?" Claudia asked.

"Don't think so," she said. "But I don't know."

"Maybe you should look in his backpack?" Claudia said. "Maybe there will be some clues in there? Maybe he left his cell phone here?"

Claudia pulled out a notebook and flipped to the first page.

"'Angel's after me, after me.'" she read softly. "'Trying to pull my strings, make me take all the drugs, money and material things. Angel don't want me to sing. Angel don't want me to sing.'"

"What the hell's that supposed to mean," Claudia said. "You know, that's interesting, cause the cops are looking for someone called Angel. You know him?"

Janice shook her head.

"You might want to tell the cops about that."

"I doubt they'd be interested in my son's bad song lyrics," Janice said.

Claudia flipped to the next page.

"'I learned one thing from my father. Honor and good intentions don't keep you alive. Medals don't matter when you're dead. The most important thing is just to survive. You gotta hide your head. Hide your head.'"

Janice's head jerked up at the words and she inhaled sharply.

"His father was a hero, you know," her voice quivered. "National Guard deployed to Iraq. Shot in the head."

An empty silence hung in the air. She didn't elaborate on the story and Claudia didn't ask.

"I probably shouldn't be reading this," Claudia said. "Seems too personal. We better get going if we are going to make it to your hearing."

When they pulled into the school parking lot, Claudia was reminded of a dungeon or a prison. There were no windows in the drab 1970s monstrosity of a building. Just a few narrow slits. They were buzzed inside and greeted by metal detectors at the entrance.

Janice didn't have a lawyer. She was armed with a purse, no briefcase. She was in her best dress, but it was a little too low cut for the occasion. To compensate, she had tossed a frumpy sweater over it.

As they checked in at the office, Claudia asked her if she wanted her to come back and pick her up when it was over.

Janice shook her head. "If you are ok staying with me, it would be nice to have somebody here," she said.

Claudia wrote her name on the sign-in sheet and the secretary told them which part of the maze-like building to head to. Claudia quickly forgot the left and rights, but Janice weaved through the hallways, passed lockers and laughing, hugging teens.

When the two entered the school board room, there was a notice on the door saying closed proceedings, executive session on disciplinary matters.

Seven grim-faced school officials greeted them glumly as they shuffled papers on their desks. A school board attorney in a tie and black suit raised his voice slightly as Janice whispered to him the situation.

"What do you mean he's not here?" the man said. "It's his responsibility to be here. We can't postpone the hearing because he didn't feel like making it out here today."

"You don't understand, sir," Janice pleaded. "He's missing. I've told the police.

"We are looking for him. We need to wait until I find him. It's not fair to expel him without hearing what he has to say. It ain't fair."

"What's not fair is wasting the board's time by not showing up. Our time is valuable, Ms. Miller," the attorney said.

"We don't even have a lawyer," Janice said.

"I assure you, Ms. Miller," he said. "Your son doesn't need a lawyer, not for this matter anyway."

"Isn't there anyone here who can speak on Kevin's defense?" Janice said. "He's a good kid. He tried hard. Got good grades."

"You received a copy of the school handbook. You are aware we have a zero-tolerance policy," the attorney said. "So we don't care about excuses, even if he was an honor student."

"How do you know it was his gun?" Janice's mouth trembled as she spoke. "How do you know he's not covering for a friend or something? That boy never so much as gets a grounding, he's so good."

"Maybe he should have gotten a grounding, Ms. Miller," the attorney said. His top lip curled back slightly as he spat the words out at her.

Claudia could see Janice's hands shaking on her lap.

"But we will hear what he told the teacher and his classmate," he said. "Ms. Williams, can you enlighten us? What happened that day?"

Ms. Williams stepped forward and played nervously with a set of keys hanging from her neck.

"Mark came up to me and said that Kevin had a gun," Ms. Williams said. "He said Kevin told him he had it for protection that someone was after him. Mark was scared something bad was going to happen to Kevin."

"So what did you do," the attorney said.

"I called the principal's office and two assistant principals and Officer Mike. We put the whole school in lockdown, got all the students locked inside the classrooms, hunched under their desks."

Claudia leaned forward on the edge of the folding metal chair.

"Kevin didn't run, just got down on the ground like Officer Mike told him and put his hands behind his back. He didn't move much and just stared down at the floor. I've had that kid in my class two years and never thought he'd be capable of bringing a gun to school. He kept yelling that he wasn't going to talk."

Janice leapt to her feet.

"Did you ever ask him what he was afraid of," Janice yelled, waving a piece of paper. "He's missing right now. Here's the police report. Something's happened to him!"

The school board members sat at the table watching intently, but didn't speak. The board president covered her mouth with her hand and leaned back in her chair.

"Ms. Miller, you need to sit down and be quiet," the attorney said. "This is not the time for you to talk."

"What about this Mark kid?" She shifted back and forth on her feet. "I want to talk to Mark. What does he have to say?"

"He's in class, Ms. Miller, and we don't need to hear what he has to say," the attorney said. "This is not a trial. It's an expulsion hearing and we have all the information we need. You're lucky your son doesn't face criminal charges for bringing a gun to school. We take this matter very seriously."

"I can't take this any more," Janice sobbed. "My son is missing and you people can't wait to expel him. You don't even care. He could be dead in a gutter somewhere. I can't listen to this anymore. I'm leaving. You don't even want to wait to hear his side of the story."

Janice scooped her purse off the floor and shook it like a dog wringing the life out of a small animal. She stormed out the room. Claudia followed her and tried to reach for her arm, but the woman was too fast.

"Janice, we will find him, OK," Claudia said. "It will be all right. He will be all right."

"I don't want to look for him right now," she said. "I just want to go home. Maybe he'll be waiting for me. Maybe he'll come back."

But her parking spot was still empty when they got back. Nothing but yellow lines, concrete and an oil stain.

"Sometimes, you feel the absence of a person just as much as their presence when they're around," Janice said. "I can just feel he isn't here.

"Usually, when I'm putting my keys in the door, I can hear the laugh-track from Kev's favorite show."

Claudia noticed it to, the empty feeling when Janice opened the door. None of the lights were on. The TV was a blank, black screen.

"No shoes and dirty socks in the middle of the hallway," Janice said.

"Do you want me to come in?" Standing at the doorstep, Claudia leaned against the heavy oak trim surrounding the front door.

"No, that's all right, but thanks for your help today," Janice said, and closed the thin door slowly behind her.

Claudia could hear the thud as Janice leaned up against the

other side. She tried not to listen but she could still hear it, the soft sound of a mother crying.

"Where's my boy?" Janice whimpered.

15 KEVIN'S SIDE OF THE STORY

Kevin had felt uneasy with the gun in his ratty backpack. He couldn't shake the feeling that the damn thing had a mind of its own, like it wanted to be seen. Looking back on that day, he couldn't think of much he'd have done differently. He needed to bring it for protection. There was no way he could've gone to school without it.

It had been surprisingly easy to get around the metal detectors with it in the bag. He had gotten around them a dozen times before. He hated waiting in line behind ten other kids having their bags searched, when they had done nothing to deserve it. He hated that the machines were the most high-tech piece of equipment in the damn school. It was such an insult, like no one believed in them enough to spend the money on textbooks or computers from the same century. In his case maybe they were right, he thought. Maybe he wasn't worth it.

The concrete walls were painted in dirty '70s hues of vomit orange and green. He had waited for the hall monitor to get distracted signing some visitor in, walked to the right and pushed through the unlocked heavy gym doors.

Some kids were playing basketball before class. Their tennis shoes squeaked against the waxed yellow floor. He had walked past them, hoping no one would slide across the white lines and bump him.

That morning, the gangbangers had been waiting for him in a car outside the front of the school. One of them was a wiry, thin guy in his 20s with blood-shot red eyes and ashy, pale skin with red splotches. Justin, a tall, lanky senior in his English class who always reeked of pot, was sitting in the back of the car. His black hair hung in greasy, unwashed streaks.

The man spoke with a low-gravelly voice through the open passenger-side window. Two girls walked by, but were too busy chatting and laughing together to hear.

"Keep your fucking mouth shut," the pale man said. "You're not a stupid kid. You'll do the right thing. And if you do talk to the cops, we'll just kill your mom. We know where you live."

"I don't want to be in the middle of this shit," Kevin said as he leaned down to the car window and eyed them. The man's hand rested on the seat and twitched. "I'm not going to say anything."

Kevin turned and walked away, across the street, wondering if shots would ring out behind him, wondering if they'd get out of the car and beat him in front of the school. He couldn't look back.

He should have felt safer with the gun in his bag, but it felt heavy and unnerving. He worried about it somehow going off, even though it was nestled in its cracked leather carrying case. Kevin didn't really want to pull it out. He didn't want to try to shoot anyone. He had never even tried to shoot a gun.

He walked across the street and passed the yellow school buses with their rumbling engines. The smell of diesel exhaust hung heavy in the air.

Maybe he would have felt less uneasy if his father had had a chance to show him how to fire it. But the man never had the time to show him how to put the safety on, how to handle it. He was too young before his father died. Kevin had had to look all that up online with the model number and the help of a couple of Youtube clips, but it wasn't reassuring.

It seemed like his mother had forgotten the gun existed, up high on the closet shelf in her bedroom, out of sight.

His hands had shook as he fumbled with the weapon in her room, but he thought he'd feel stronger with it nearby, knowing he could pull it out if he had to. He was trying to be responsible about it.

He walked across the open cafeteria, past the tables and plastic benches and saw the school police officer hitting the buttons on the vending machine.

He had stared at the officer's gun, hanging off his hip in a black holster. He was a round man stuffed into a black corset, a bullet-proof vest. Kevin started to walk toward him. He wanted to talk, maybe it was the only way, but there was Justin, watching him from across the room with his eyes in narrow slits.

Kevin's stomach felt like it was filled with acid. His breath came out in tight, little spurts. It seemed like they were just waiting to catch him alone, like that was the only reason he was not dead yet. It was just a matter of time before they'd follow him home on his way back from school. They had been hassling him for months.

He had sighed and kept walking to class. He jumped at the sound of a locker slamming behind him.

In the classroom, he dropped the heavy bag to the floor and tried to listen as the gray-haired geometry teacher explained how to calculate the circumference of a circle. Kevin was usually good at geometry and he liked Mr. Olsen, but it didn't make sense when he kept tuning out every other word.

Kevin flinched when Mr. Olsen hurled a piece of chalk at the blackboard. White fragments flew in different directions. The teacher gave Kevin his most theatrically gruff expression. "Are you listening, Kevin?" he said.

"Yeah, of course," he had said. He swallowed and leaned forward in his desk, putting his arms around it. It was like he was lost at sea and holding onto a piece of wooden wreckage. He wrapped one arm around his notebook and hunched down over the lined paper, scribbling song lyrics and bowing down his head.

"Angel don't want me to sing," he wrote. "Angel don't want me to sing."

A moment before the bell rang, he stuffed the notebook into his bag and Mark, the preppy kid sitting next to him, saw the gun in the leather case. Kevin swallowed. It was like the gun wanted to be seen.

"Listen, I can explain," he said. Mark shuffled off and tried to avoid eye contact.

"It's for protection, Mark." Kevin said. "I swear. Someone's after me."

"Ok," Mark said and walked briskly down the hallway.

Fuck, Kevin thought. Within five minutes, the fat cop had him pinned down with his face against the shiny, gray hallway floor, twisting his wrists behind his back. The floor tasted of drool, dirty shoes and bleach as his mouth crushed against it.

Justin watched as they pulled Kevin out the door and for a moment, the two of them locked eyes.

"You have the right to remain silent…" the cop spouted.

"I'm not gonna say nothing!" Kevin yelled. "I'm not gonna say nothing!"

Kevin squished his eyes closed and silently prayed they'd believe him.

As the cop pulled him to his feet and dragged him out the door, he looked over his shoulder to glimpse Justin pulling out his cell phone and punching in a text.

Kevin decided he wasn't going to talk. He wasn't lying when he said he wouldn't say anything. He'd go to jail if he had to. It would be a relief.

How disappointing it was when they let him go home with his mother, pending possible criminal charges.

16 WANTED FOR MURDER

A month after the expulsion hearing, the police finally seemed to be looking for Kevin, but Janice wasn't happy about it. He was wanted for questioning about the murder.

Tom and Claudia were sitting on the couch watching the TV news when his photo flashed across the screen. It was a yearbook photo but somehow it looked like a classic mug shot complete with bad hair and bewildered blood-shot eyes. Janice's car had been found parked downtown. It was towed from a loading zone near the bus and train stations. Police suspected he had fled the state.

"Police are not calling him a suspect in the case, at this time," the TV newswoman said, with weird inflections in her voice. It certainly didn't sound like she believed it.

"Bullshit he's not a suspect," Tom said, turning off the TV. "That's why he's on the run."

"How do you know?" Claudia said. "He's a kid, Tom. Maybe he's in trouble somewhere."

"He's 17, sweetheart. That's close enough to act like a man."

"Sweetheart? Since when did you start calling me sweetheart? You're starting to sound like Stan."

"Like a chauvinistic, old cop?"

"He's not that much older than you," Claudia said, crossing her arms.

"Whatever," Tom said, smiling. "I just like to get a rise out of you, sometimes. Makes life more interesting, picking on your roommate."

"On that thought, have you painted anything today?" she asked, changing the subject. She noticed Tom had ridges of blue and green underneath dirty nails and faint remnants of paint lining his knuckles.

"Yes," he said. "But I'm not showing it to you. It's not finished."

"I'm going to go with Janice to help put up more fliers," she said.

"You're probably just wasting your time," Tom said. "He's fine. He's probably out there with his friends, having a grand old time."

"I hope so," she said. "I really do."

When Claudia showed up to help Janice, she had two large bags of fliers and Alice by her side. The three of them walked all around the neighborhood putting up fliers with Kevin's photo on them and stuffed fliers in mailboxes. He looked much happier in these photos. He was jamming out with his guitar and had a smile on his face. The fliers had all the usual data. Name: Kevin Miller. Height: 5'11. Weight: 270. Age: 17. Last seen date: 5/09. Jesus, Claudia thought, she hadn't realized he was 270 pounds.

Janice was quiet as she stapled the sheets to the wooden poles down the street and ducked inside businesses to tape fliers on the insides of windows.

Alice handed Janice a piece of tape. "There's something I have to tell you," she said.

The three of them stopped and took a break, sitting on the curb and passing the same water bottle back and forth. Claudia tried not to let the plastic touch her lips and spilled a bit down her chin and shirt.

"Janice, it's really hard for me to tell you this but I think you should know," Alice said. "Maybe it will help you come to grips with the situation, I don't know. If I were in your place, I'd want to know."

"Know what?" Janice said.

"Well, two things. One is that your son is a suspect in that murder." Alice tucked a lock of blond hair behind her ear and nervously bit her nails.

"No he isn't." Janice's mouth formed a grim, straight line.

"Yes, he is."

"How do you know that?"

"Because I've talked with the police about what's going on," she said. "He kind of confided in me. I told the police what he said. I had to. I wouldn't call it a confession, but he kind of hinted that he had done something he regretted."

"What do you mean, confession?" Janice threw up her hands and then placed them on her hips. "That's news to me."

"I was talking to him about God," Alice said softly. She placed her hand gently on Janice's shoulder. "We started having some conversations before he disappeared. You saw us together. He said he had done something terribly wrong and he regretted it. He never told me exactly what it was, but he didn't need to."

Janice stood up and shook Alice's arm off of hers. "Get away from me. You lying bitch. My son's innocent. My son would never… My son would never ever do that. I begged him to tell me what was bothering him. I begged him and he wouldn't and you think he'd tell you?"

Janice started crying and pushing the tears away with her hands.

"He said he was a sinner," Alice mumbled softly. "I think he just wanted some peace. He said he couldn't bear to tell you. At least, he's accepted Christ into his heart. I know it's hard and I'm worried about him too, but maybe you can at least find a little comfort in that he's trying to get on the right path now. I'm just trying to do the right thing. Should I have kept that information from the police?"

Janice walked down the block, swinging her arms wildly behind her.

Alice didn't get up, but sat slumped forward a bit, from her perch on the curb. She bent her head and heaved a deep breath. "I just pray God will take care of that kid, you know." She wiped her eyes. "He's just so young. You just can't win."

Then she lifted her blue eyes to the heavens and let her lips curl around the water bottle in one last swig.

"It's so sad," Alice said, twisting the bottle in her hands. "Look at how out of control Janice is right now. I feel bad, but I couldn't not tell her."

"Maybe it will help Janice understand what's going on," Claudia said with a sigh. "She needs to accept it. She thinks that boy is an angel and the fact is he's not."

Alice picked up one of the fliers with Kevin's picture and stared at it for a moment. She folded it neatly in half and slid it into her designer purse.

"Maybe I should scan it and put it on Facebook," she mumbled. "Maybe that would help us find the kid."

17 RUNNING

Kevin had been on the Greyhound bus for only four hours before the eight-year-old girl started throwing up next to him. The vomit hit the aisle with a series of splats and guttural sounds. He checked his pant legs but didn't see any chunks, just an orange spot or two on the top of his right sock.

"You ok?" he asked, looking up.

The girl nodded, wiped her mouth and went over to sit on her mom's lap.

"I'm not supposed to talk to strangers," she whispered.

It was the first time he was headed to his grandfather's house voluntarily. It was always so damn cold there at Christmas, he hated visiting and his mom never got along with her family. Even as a five-year-old, he could feel the unease in the pit of his stomach when he tried to sleep in the old house with its creepy, vine-covered wallpaper. He'd drink a glass of water, thinking he was thirsty, but the feeling wouldn't go away.

But there was always one place he felt safe, by the fireplace watching the flames feast on wrapping paper. He loved the warmth on his back as he reached for the next present in front of him.

Would it be better there without his mom? His grandfather

loved to break all the rules when he was a kid. He always let Kevin do whatever he wanted, stay up late, sit around in pajamas all day, skip the toothbrush, drink pop until the cans piled up and play cards for hours. He'd miss his videogames, but at least no one would know where he was. He didn't think his grandfather even knew his mom's number anymore. The two had fought bitterly over his grandmother's death.

He sighed thinking about his mom and shifted in his seat.

"Why did you take the gun to school?" his mom had said. "I love you. You need to tell me what's going on. What happened? I need to understand so I can help you."

"Mom, you won't understand," he told her hours before he left. "I ain't a snitch. I ain't talking to the police. Do you know what they'd do to me? They'd kill me."

"You can make a right choice or a wrong choice," his mom had yelled.

"I ain't a snitch," he yelled.

"You're a coward," she yelled back. "What would your father think of you?"

He thought of the rage in her eyes, how her chin had trembled and her lips had curled back as she said it.

Kevin gulped the hurt down just thinking about it.

He tried not to think about the funeral, the American flag draped over the coffin, the box of glinting medals and the flowers spilling across the floor. His father served his country, not his family. Kevin knew it was wrong of him to think that thought, but he couldn't help it when he was listening to all the patriotic bullshit from the podium. Where was the man when he needed him? The man chose to give his life away instead of giving it to them.

They were halfway there. Kevin stared at the rolling green hills, the bloated black and white cows with muddy bellies. He could smell the shit.

"Mom, it's better if you don't know," he had told her.

Was he wrong to leave her behind? What protection could he really provide her without a gun anyway? His mom would be ok. They had no reason to bother her with him gone.

But he still felt that feeling in the bottom of his stomach. He was thirsty. That was it. He needed water. He pulled the plastic bottle out from the seat back in front of him. It was half-squashed, but there was still a bit in the bottom. He unscrewed the cap with his thick fingers and sucked back the last drops until the plastic bottle started to collapse onto itself. The feeling was still there.

He squashed the bottle and dropped it on the ground where it rolled back and forth against his feet. It was better than putting it in the pocket in front of him considering his shins were already jammed up against the seat back. He was even bigger than his father. The man would've kicked his ass for losing his gun.

He could've talked, he thought.

Maybe he should go back. Maybe he should talk to the police. Kevin could sit down with his mom and tell them everything. Frankly, he didn't care about school anymore. He didn't care about anything but living. Kevin didn't want to be like his father. He didn't want to give his life away.

He stared at the faded fabric on the seat back in front of him with its ugly orange and purple geometric pattern. Kevin tried not to think of anything anymore. He put his headphones in his ears but didn't turn the music on. He didn't feel like it. He just listened to the squeak of brakes, that groan buses make as they accelerate from a stop. They were pulling into the stop-and-go rush hour traffic of the city. He stared at the small, sharp skyline of St. Paul and felt a growing sense of uneasiness as the bus exited onto slow residential streets.

He walked down the dirty steps and out into the swinging glass doors of the bus station. He pulled his bag close to him and sat in an orange, bucket seat. Everyone else was being hugged and escorted out by friends or family.

A cop with a muzzled German shepherd walked by him. Wet streaks ran across the concrete floor and he thought he smelled the faint scent of someone else's urine on his damp seat. He switched to the next one over.

What now, he thought. What do I do now?

Kevin had left his cell phone at home, afraid they'd somehow track him with it.

He reached into his bag and untied the sock full of coins he brought with him. He felt foolish but every bit counted on the run and the sock had 48 dollars and 17 cents in it. He could also use it as a weapon if he had to and hit someone with the sack of metal. He inserted one of the quarters into an old pay phone. It felt foreign to hold the hollow plastic receiver up to his ear, like a reminder of a different world. He turned the metal knob and his quarter disappeared into the museum piece. Then a dime disappeared but nothing happened.

He didn't want to spend all his money on a cab, so he decided to walk. It was only a few miles. Kevin kept adjusting the strap on his duffel bag every few blocks. It just kept sinking further and further into his shoulder.

The extra weight on his legs and arms rubbed against the sweaty fabric of his clothes, but he didn't care. This city felt green and lush and clean. The air tasted different. Walking was like a kind of meditation. It calmed the panic and worry that had grown in his mind on the long bus ride. Even the pain growing in his shoulder, where the bag strap cut in, felt welcome. It was a physical distraction from the worry.

He worried that he'd forget which block the house was on. He worried that he'd knock and no one would answer.

Kevin recognized the house right away. It was an old ranch-style home from the 1950s, with faded siding on the triangle above the doorway, and a diamond shaped window on the front door. The grass jutted out in tall tufts between tangles of creeping Charlie and its small purplish flowers.

Kevin only spent a moment on the doorstep before the door swung open. He hadn't even knocked or run the bell.

The man was smaller than he remembered. His grandfather seemed to have shrunk. Through the lines, he recognized his mother's light brown eyes peering at him.

"Nice to see you, Kev," he said. "How the hell you doin' these days?"

"Ok, how about you?"

"Fine, just fine," he said, but Kevin could tell he was lying by the fact he didn't look him in the eye.

"Come inside. You must be thirsty."

He sat down at his kitchen table and continued drinking a Miller Lite, while Kevin poured himself some water into a slightly brown glass. There were a dozen cans scattered around the kitchen and a row of prescription pill bottles laid out in front of his grandfather on the table.

Some of the bottles were clearly marked with warnings in big type – do not consume alcohol while taking this medication.

"Why you drinking that?" Kevin asked, pointing to the can.

"Oh, I figure the light version is better for my health, you know," his grandfather said dryly, patting his large stomach. "Gotta watch the beer belly. You want one?"

"No, thanks," Kevin said, sitting back and sipping his water. He noticed the recycle bin in the corner of the kitchen was bursting with a tower of squashed beer cans.

His mother would have said something. His grandmother would have said something, too. But Kevin knew better.

His grandmother had been dead for years, but her knickknacks were still growing thick, furry dust coats on a shelf on the wall. The memory of how she died still drove a wedge between his mother and his grandfather. His grandmother hated hospitals and his grandfather had followed her wishes up to the end and refused to hospitalize her. His mother had called him a drunk and swore she would never talk to him again and he had swore the same back at her and yelled that people had a right to choose how they want to die. They hadn't spoken since.

"What do you do all day, Grandpa?" Kevin asked.

"Watch TV, drink beer," the old man said. "Play solitaire. I like 'Wheel of Fortune.' Miss 'Price is Right.' It's just not the same without Bob Barker.

"I hate it when people die," he added. "It seems like all my friends are kicking the bucket."

"You know what you need, dude?"

Kevin leaned back in his chair so the front legs lifted of the ground.

"What?"

"The Nintendo Wii," Kevin said, smiling. "Old people love it."

His grandfather gave him a playful slap on the arm for the comment. "The Nintendo wee wee?" he said. "What's that?"

"The Wii. It's a videogame, dude. What, you live in a cave?"

"Does this look like Afghanistan? How about you?" his grandfather said opening his arms wide with his palms up. "Where are you living?"

"I was going to ask you about that," Kevin said nervously.

"Ah huh, I knew it," his grandfather said, slapping the kitchen table in front of him. "Show up here a week after my birthday and you want something from me. You want to live here, huh, things not going so hot with your mom?

"I always said you and your mom should live here. I could've helped out with takin' care of you while your dad was out in Iraq and then after your grandma... But she didn't listen."

"So I can stay here, then?"

"Sure, kid." His grandfather took a swig of his beer.

"Thanks, man! Happy birthday," Kevin said. "Sorry I missed it."

"I missed yours, too," his grandfather said, frowning. "It was in May, wasn't it?"

"January, actually."

"Hmm. Maybe we should get ourselves some presents. I haven't seen you in what, four years, so I owe interest, right? Let's go get this wee wee thing you talked about."

He winked and grabbed his keys off the rack with surprising speed for a man his age, especially after an unknown number of Miller Lites.

"Grandpa, can I drive? I just got my license and I could use the practice." Kevin lied. He hadn't had a chance to take the exam yet, but it seemed the lesser of two evils.

When they got back and Kevin was fiddling with the cables

behind the ancient TV set, his grandfather turned the thing onto the news, put on his glasses and squinted.

Kevin didn't usually pay much attention to the news, but he found himself staring down at the screen from a funny angle while he worked and unwrapped the pieces of the videogame system, ripping plastic bags and Styrofoam.

The newscaster with his hair perfectly coifed and hair-sprayed into a wave, sat grim-faced talking in a serious tone about a gang-related shooting.

"Police believe the teen was not gang affiliated and was shot dead in a case of mistaken identity," he read with his eyes glued dramatically into the camera.

"Goddamn terrorists!" his grandfather shouted, shaking his cane at the TV.

The newscaster had taken a long dramatic pause so he was uninterrupted. "Two suspects have been charged with first-degree murder and felony drug possession. Sources say they were carrying large amounts of meth."

Kevin shuddered looking at the dead kid's picture. He was only 15 and he looked an awful lot like him.

"Police have also released a sketch of a third suspect who fled the scene." His grandfather stared at it, sitting forward in his seat.

Then Kevin plugged in the last of the cables and the picture went black. It was time to play.

18 LADY JUSTICE

Every now and then Tom would go to Sara Johnson's hearings about his attempted stabbing. Claudia came with him occasionally.

They sat in the gray, plastic chairs next to all the other witnesses and relatives, fenced in behind the armed guards and a wooden railing, waiting for the judge to arrive.

"You know if you stare at that small blindfolded statue holding the scales long enough, you start to imagine things," Tom whispered to Claudia.

"You fantasize about lady justice?" Claudia laughed. An old man sitting next to her turned away slightly in his chair.

"I used to stare so hard I'd imagine she started to move," Tom said, pointing to the small statue. "She'd put down her scales and walk slowly out onto the street, tapping a cane in front of her against the sidewalk, tap, tap, tapping. It takes her an awful long time to find the answers that way."

Claudia raised her eyebrows at him. "Just how much time have you spent in courtrooms?" she asked.

She shifted her gaze as the judge walked in. The procession started and the small crowd hushed down into silence. The offenders were paraded in front of them, and Mrs. Johnson's case was no different.

The prosecutor and the attorney shuffled up to the podium with their piles of papers clipped together.

As they opened their mouths, Claudia always expected them to say something important, something earth shattering, like "Law and Order." She would expect them to move forward swiftly and to reach a conclusion in 60 minutes with commercial breaks but instead they'd start talking about their vacations.

"I'm available the week of June 16,"

"No good for me, I'm scheduled to be out of the office on a fishing trip," one of the lawyers said.

"How about the week of July 5?"

"No good," the judge said instead. "I'm out most of July."

"How about August then?"

Her stomach sank deeper into the plastic chair. Each hearing date was only meant to set another hearing date. Nothing else was discussed and no real progress was made. But papers were pushed around and calendars were consulted. It was all very important.

The only important thing that actually happened was in the first hearing when Mrs. Johnson was let out on bail. The woman in the courtroom was professional looking, wearing a black suit and light blue dress shirt, and towering in high heels. Her sleek, red ponytail swished playfully behind her as she turned her head to stare at Tom with blank, wide eyes.

Claudia asked Tom if he was afraid and squeezed his hand. He laughed at her. But she noticed after that that he kept a hammer in his room, with the dust bunnies under his bed. Had it always been there?

She kept thinking about the medical examiner's statement in the news article, "blunt force trauma to the head." It could've been a hammer. It could have been a lot of things.

19 BEHIND THE LOCKS

Tom kept his room locked when he was working. He didn't want her to see what he was up to. It seemed to give him the equivalent of writer's block for painters. Painter's block.

But Claudia was a snoop by nature and admitted it. He knew this about her, so she didn't feel guilty about going into his room that day. If he left his door unlocked that was his problem. He'd know it was fair game, she thought. Wouldn't he?

He had left the window open with the curtains billowing next to his bed. The sheets were crumpled and twisted in a way that made it look like someone had hidden a body under them, Claudia thought. She let her imagination get away from her sometimes.

She pulled the hammer out from under the bed and looked for specks of blood in the cracks on the handle.

Holding the heavy hammer, it struck her that she cared for Tom but until she had answers about his past she couldn't do anything about it.

Finding nothing, not a hair, not a faint touch of red, she slipped it back under the bed into the dust. He always kept his tools clean, whether it was a hammer or a paintbrush. She was being paranoid, she told herself.

Claudia was having one of those creative days when her mind wandered, when she felt like a ghost looking back at her life. It was one of those days when each ray of sunshine coming in through the window seemed so brilliantly bright she just wanted to can it and save it for a dark moment. It was one of those days when she heard music in her head, like an imaginary jam session between the dead, Janis Joplin and Jimi Hendrix. It was one of those days when she needed more sleep, when she was half stuck in a dream.

She found herself humming and going through Tom's things in an absent-minded state. Crumpled boxers, dirty socks and T-shirts littered the floor. A pair of jeans sat waiting with crumpled legs upright in a short pile, like he just slipped them off and left two denim holes behind. An alarm clock hid behind the stack of murder mysteries on the nightstand.

In the corner, there was an easel with his latest creation. Paint tubes were lined up on a table next to it. She picked them up and noticed the spotless labels, burnt sunset, cayenne red, forest green and ocean blue.

"I've got a terrible secret," Tom whispered into her ear.

Claudia froze and her heart stammered as he placed his hands on her shoulders and stood behind her. Jesus Christ, is he going to kill me, she wondered.

"What is it?" she said.

"Can you guess?" he said. "Take a good look at the picture. "Does something seem a little off to you?"

She leaned forward and stared at the painting, mostly in black and white with touches of color here and there. It was a woman in gray scale with bright blue eyes and a full, blood red lips and purple hair.

"She's beautiful, of course," she said. "The colors seem a little off, gives a feeling of discord to the piece."

Tom often just picked one color and painted in shades of it. That was his signature style, but it also got him in trouble with critics.

"It's nice to see you branch out," she said.

"Does she look like anyone you know?" he asked.

"I don't know anyone with purple hair," Claudia said.

"Damn it." He crossed his arms.

She breathed out.

What are you doing in my room, anyway?"

"The door was open. I was just looking for the scissors. I can never find anything."

"They're in the drawer."

"No they aren't. I looked there already."

Tom walked back to the kitchen and pulled open the drawer, rattling all the knives and spatulas as they slid forward.

"They're right there," he said. "You're hopeless. You never see what's right in front of you."

Claudia didn't say anything, but she knew exactly what he meant. Her good friend and roommate Tom, who she kept telling her mother was like a brother to her, wasn't like a brother at all.

The woman in the picture was another version of her, but she had no idea what she wanted to do about it. Maybe this was normal when you live with an artist, to be turned into a subject, she thought. But something told her no.

For a moment she was haunted by Steve Jackson. A small warning sounded in her stomach that it was dangerous to trust anyone who might have done it, however unlikely. She wanted answers and Kevin's impending arrest was not enough.

In reality, she still couldn't imagine Tom killing someone so it was irrational not to trust him. But it would be reckless to get involved with a man with a criminal record, reckless and stupid. Then again, she was already living with him.

But when she looked at Tom, all she saw was someone standing by her when times were hard, her best friend in the whole world. She didn't want to screw it up. That was the real fear.

So she said nothing. Judging by his scowl, it was the worst thing to say at all.

20 DIVINE LOVE

One of the benefits of unemployment was Claudia had plenty of time to attempt jogging. She wondered how long it would take her to run a mile these days.

One of her tennis shoes squeaked in a slow steady rhythm as she loped through the neighborhood. She lost track of the blocks as she passed rows of houses and humming lawn mowers. It was 83 degrees and the wisps of hair frothed around her face. She stopped and wiped the sweat and hair back, leaned down to touch her toes and took deep slow breaths. Maybe this was a bad idea.

She started to walk, feeling the side stitch climb up her gut. Up ahead, she spotted the four giant Roman pillars of an old, abandoned church and wondered if it was the church Alice was working on. It looked like the picture in the brochure but in worse shape. She sat down on the crumbling steps.

Claudia had had enough of her talk of divine love and yet she couldn't seem to escape it. The walls were covered with tendrils of half-dead ivy snaking across the stone and yet she could still make out the inscription. "Divine love always has met and always will meet every human need" – Mary Eddy Baker.

Who was she and what would she think of these ruins?

Claudia wondered. What would she think of the crumbling stairs leading to chains on weathered wooden doors, the rusted railing, and the broken panes of glass? Vacant homes littered the block.

The house of God was all boarded up with a no trespassing sign hanging on its doors. Above the doorway, pigeon spikes adorned decorative baskets of stone fruit, like old Christmas lights left up long after the season was over.

Vacant lots formed a small urban prairie around the building with tall grass and wildflowers bowing with the wind. Many of the posts holding up the chain link fence had toppled, leaving slouching metal borders in between.

After a slow walk home and a shaky ascent up the stairs to their apartment, Claudia swung open the door.

Tom immediately sniffed the air. He was sitting on the couch with a remote in each hand.

"You stink," he said playfully with a smirk and turned off the TV. "I can smell you all the way from here. What were you doing out there?"

"You should be proud of me. I got my lazy ass off the couch and ran all the way to the old church, the one Alice's always talking about."

"I'd like to see the inside of that building," he said. "I think I dream about it. Do you think it's really the way I dream it?"

She sighed. "Who would believe you if it were?" she said.

"I've already started painting it. I think I have anyway, you never know for sure. It could always be a different old church somewhere else," he said. "We could go over there and take a look. I'll bet you a hundred bucks."

"You know I don't have that kind of money," she said.

"I accept other forms of payment," Tom said, wiggling his eyebrows up and down. "Just kidding, but not really."

"I don't know if I should take that bet," she said. "If you've seen one old church, you've seen them all, haven't you?"

Later that day, they drove by the old church and couldn't help but stare. Men in grubby work clothes streamed in and out the back entrances. The front wooden doors were still chained closed, but they could see the dusty footprints going around the back. Piles of wood and junk overflowed from the dumpster at the side of the old brick and stone building. Old wooden chairs were stacked by the dumpster, as well as pieces of wood trim with the paint peeling off.

From the outside, no progress had been made, but Claudia could feel something had changed. It had a different vibe. The building was no longer abandoned and dying. There was a new, mysterious life breathing inside it. The smell of paint and chemicals hung in the air.

Two days later, Claudia found Tom in the hallway talking with Alice. He had his arm against the wall and the two of them were laughing in a nervous way.

"Why won't you let me see it?" he pleaded.

"I will eventually when it's open to the public," she said, smiling. "But right now it's not really all that safe and it's covered in peeling plaster and paint. After the contractors found the asbestos, things got complicated. They make it sound like we've got building inspections every other day."

"What if I volunteer? I could help paint the inside. Interior paint isn't that different from oils and acrylics. I'm good with a brush. Maybe I could restore some of the old artwork, too?"

"To be honest, I haven't even been allowed inside for more than a month," she said. "It's just the contractors in their masks at this point. It seems like it's going to take an eternity, but I'll let you know when they say it's OK to have people back in."

Alice gave a nervous laugh and shot an exasperated glance in Claudia's direction.

"Thanks for the offer," she said. "I'll let you know when your services are needed. There will come a time."

"How long do you think it will take? I've got a running bet with Claudia about what it looks like on the inside."

"Might be months or a few years," she said. "A lot depends on how structurally sound it is. But I can't go having you falling through floor boards and breaking your neck, especially a nice neighbor like you."

"I promise I won't sue," Tom said, winking.

"I really can't," she said, smiling. "You have no idea how high the insurance is and the liability."

Once they got back into their apartment, Tom showed Claudia the canvas and frowned.

"It really is driving me nuts," he said. "I know it shouldn't look like this but I keep seeing it this way. I have to see the inside."

Broken glass, pigeon shit and kitty litter at the feet of a shrugging, open-armed bleeding Jesus Christ.

"He looks like a heroin addict or something," she said.

"I know," Tom said. "Do you think I'm going to hell for painting it?"

"Maybe," Claudia said, patting his arm. "You are a twisted soul."

21 TED'S WEAPON

Claudia spotted Ted, the building manager, washing down the porches. He smiled as he sloshed the water through the wooden planks and reloaded his weapon of choice – an old plastic bucket.

Ted didn't like Doris much, after too many years of getting cranky phone calls of complaints. She was perpetually telling him he missed a spot vacuuming the rug in the hallway, that her apartment was too hot or too cold and that he was somehow legally responsible for the legions of ladybugs infesting her bedroom window. He'd go in to inspect and she'd wave a lone insect carcass around and yell, "I'm going to sue you for everything!"

Maybe that's why he so eagerly sloshed water down three stories worth of porches, drenching her laundry on the line, a faded dress, an old pair of jeans and a souvenir T-shirt with a picture of Niagara Falls.

"Theodore, for God's sake, no!" Doris yelled.

"Didn't you see the notice?" he said, cursing under his breath in Spanish. "Porch washing time. And it's Teodoro, by the way."

The water flowed in the gaps in between the boards like a waterfall. It was not the first time Tom and Claudia had heard the sloshing and the outcry. They always chuckled at the exchange between Ted with his vengeful buckets full of water and angry protests from Doris.

Claudia ran down to Ted and told him she had a bunch of pots she'd like to put in the basement but had misplaced her key.

"Do you think you could let me in?" she asked.

"Sure," he said, grinning mischievously.

She grabbed the dirty plastic pots from her back porch and followed him into the dingy basement.

"There's something about a basement in a building that's more than a hundred years old that makes you want to wear a gas mask," she mumbled.

The smells of mold and old decaying bricks assailed them as they walked in. The windows were covered in cobwebs and the brick wall was coated with a mysterious flaky white substance. Shovels and shears leaned up against it. In the corners, black boxes waited for rats to slip inside their black holes to feast on a last free meal.

"It's always so creepy down here," Claudia said, tossing the pots in her rickety section of basement storage, a small room constructed of spare planks of wood. Anyone could see through the gaps. She didn't bother to lock it, since there was nothing of value, just an old, broken washing machine and a pair of old skis from the 1970s she inexplicably pulled out of a dumpster. Anything nicer than that would just get covered in muddy rat prints anyway, she thought.

She inhaled sharply as Ted reached for a pair of rusty shears. He was not tall, but he was imposing. His calf muscles cut sharp lines into his legs as he started to scale the stairs out of the basement. Hulky shoulders blocked the sunlight as he stood in the doorway.

"I don't remember having a shovel in here," Claudia mumbled as she reached for the flimsy door handle.

"What was that? Hey, is that one of mine?" Ted said. "I've been missing one since that snowstorm in January."

Claudia grabbed the orange handle and pulled it out of

107

the room, holding it just below the bent metal blade.

"I don't know how it got in here," she said.

"How'd it end up in your storage unit, then?" Ted raised his eyebrows and walked back toward her. "I haven't seen this one since that big snowstorm, around the time that guy died. Damn pain in the ass trying dig out the sidewalks without it. Maybe you borrowed it to dig out your car and didn't put it back?"

"I didn't take it," she said.

"Sure," Ted mumbled. "You know, people take the weirdest things in this building. Someone likes to take all the light bulbs from the basement. I never bother putting in energy efficient ones anymore."

"Do you put in any? It's so dark in here," she said. "Where do you want me to put it?"

"Up against the wall." He shrugged.

The sunlight from the doorway fell on the bent metal shovel. Claudia gasped as she caught sight of a tuft of hair and dried brown blood stuck to the edge.

"Ted." She said.

"What?"

"Look." She pointed to the crusted blood crowning the blade. "Maybe this was the murder weapon? We need to call the cops."

"You call 'em," he said. "I don't wanna talk to them."

He left the basement and started clipping a scraggly bush by the parking lot.

"Ted, why don't you want to talk to the cops?" she said.

"I don't like police," Ted said. "I don't trust 'em."

"Why not?" She put her hands on her hips. "What are you scared of?"

"I just don't like 'em," Ted said.

Claudia looked at Ted, and his stocky, muscular frame as he clipped the hedges, with a snip, snip, snap. It was easy to imagine him in a horror movie using the shears to snap off someone's head. She backed off and called the cops.

Stan looked incredulous when she told him. "Really?" he said. "You're just noticing it now? Where was it exactly?"

She pointed to the corner near the shelf.

"Doesn't look like they could have slid it through the openings in between the slats and have it stand upright against the wall," he said. "Who else has the key?"

"Tom does," she said, noticing the way Stan eyed her as she said the name. "But I don't actually keep it locked. It's just junk."

"Am I a suspect now?" she said.

"Everyone's a suspect, dear," he said. "But what do you think? Should you be?"

"It's weird that I discover the body and six months later, the murder weapon. But if I were the killer, I wouldn't be calling you about it, now would I?"

"Exactly, sweetheart," Stan said. "But of course, you never know."

Claudia told Tom how it all happened when she got back into the apartment. He was surfing the Internet but slapped the laptop shut when he saw her face as she opened the door. Her mouth was contorted in a grimace and her eyes narrowed under heavy eyebrows.

"How do you spot the face of a murderer?" Claudia let out an exasperated breath.

"People talk about feminine intuition all the time," he said, putting an arm around her tight shoulders. "What does yours tell you?"

Her muscles tightened even more with his touch.

"Feminine intuition is a load of bull shit," she said. "No one ever figured out a murder based on feminine intuition. Not in real life."

But she closed her eyes for a moment, took a deep breath and tried to channel what little she had. It just made her angry there were no answers.

"You wanna know what my 'feminine intuition' says?" Tom said, taking a sip of a warm bottle of beer left on the coffee table. "Maybe it's Ted's immigration status that makes him wary of the police. I've got nothing against the man personally."

"I just thought it was odd that he didn't want to talk to the cops," she said. "But at least he didn't run away. I still wonder about Kevin."

Claudia leaned up against Tom, relieved the hammer had nothing to do with it. She had nothing to be afraid of. She could be safe with him now, couldn't she?

She went into her room and called Stan's number. She asked him a simple question about Tom.

"If it was a juvenile record, why did you tell me about it?" she said. "I thought police weren't supposed to talk about juvenile records. It's sealed right?"

"Oh honey," he said. "Is that what he told you? Tom's a felon. You can look up his record at the Cook County courthouse if you like. It's public record."

Claudia got off the phone, her face burning red. It wasn't time for a conversation anymore. It was time to move. Too bad moving wasn't so simple. She resigned herself to pretending that everything was ok, keeping her mouth shut for a while, until she could figure things out. Where the hell was she going to go?

22 GAME'S OVER

Kevin crushed the Miller Lite cans and tried not to count them as he tossed them into a plastic bag. Had Grandpa always drank this much? Had he just never noticed or had it gotten worse after his father died? It was hard to tell.

He carried the bag out of the house and noticed it dripping yellow, stale booze onto his Nikes. He couldn't help but swear since they were the only shoes he had. Great, now everyone is going to smell me and think I'm an alcoholic, he mumbled.

But who besides his grandfather was really seeing or smelling him anyway. The two of them were constantly holed up playing the "wee wee" as his grandfather creepily called it. Kevin would take what he could for entertainment.

When his grandfather would hobble off to the bathroom, Kevin would sometimes dump out the old man's beer into a half-dead potted plant and replace it with a glass of water. His grandfather would take a sip, give him a look, but the old man never said nothing.

Maybe it was because the water helped his game. His cane sat up against the old, olive green chair and the man stood up, swinging his arms wildly and shouting at the screen. Or maybe it was because he wasn't alone anymore.

It didn't matter what game they played, he was kicking

Kevin's ass and laughing about it. As the weeks went on, the potted plant in the corner got lusher and greener.

"I haven't actually bowled in 20 years," his grandpa said. "No, more like 30. I used to belong to a league, you know."

Kevin set down his white controller and stared out the window at the tall, tangled weeds.

"Grandpa, you want me to mow?" Kevin asked.

"You tired of defeat?" the old man, chuckled.

"Nah, I just thought maybe I should do something to help around here."

"Good, boy," his grandfather said. "You should earn your keep. At least your mom taught you something right."

But the mower wouldn't start. It took Kevin a while to find the gasoline in the garage. He knocked over a rusty rake and cut his hand. He had to move the remains of three mangled bicycles just to get to the can. It was obvious his grandfather had run over them a few times judging by the twisted tires. Had he been drinking at the time?

Kevin poured the gurgling gasoline into the mower, pulled the cord and was off. The only times he ever mowed grass was at his grandfather's house when he was a kid. It seemed exotic at the time. At home, there was no grass to mow, no backyard – just a lot of concrete in the parking lot. Now, Kevin smelled the scent of cut grass and dirt, and watched his Nikes take on a faint green hue, as he chopped rows of short grass up and down the lawn.

A white van stopped in front of the house. At first, Kevin didn't think anything of it. He didn't notice them staring at him. Then, the little hairs on the back of his neck started to stand up, despite the sweat. They weren't getting out of the car. They were just sitting there looking at him.

He stopped the lawnmower and rolled it back into the garage.

He walked back into the house slowly, trying not to look over his shoulder, trying not to stare back. But then the men flung open the door and started running after him.

Back when Kevin was in second grade and teachers talked

about stranger danger, he always thought it didn't matter if someone chased him. He could always get away. He would summon an extra burst of energy. The danger would boost his speed and no one would ever be able to catch him.

But the fact of the matter was, the extra pounds were too heavy for him to spring like a gazelle across the lawn into his home, and the men grabbed him by the arm just as his fingers reached for the doorknob. They pushed him inside the house.

Grandpa was waiting.

23 ANGEL OF DEATH

The phone rang. Tom, shirtless as always, answered then sank down onto a chair.

"Really? Someone wants to buy it? For $1,000? This afternoon? I'll come by."

He put down the phone and clapped his hands together loudly.

"Paul says someone wants to buy the reaper for $1,000 bucks," he hooted.

He gave Claudia an awkward hug before she could pull away.

Tom scrambled to find a clean shirt off his bedroom floor, and finally dug out the white one from his closet. As his fingers danced over the buttons, he asked Claudia if she wanted to join him for a drink.

"Sure," she said, smiling despite herself. "Sounds like you're buying."

She put on mascara and paused to look at herself in the mirror. It was a nice tight, black shirt, but not enough cleavage for a bar, she thought, so she went back to her room and hoisted herself into a different bra. She forgot to close the door all the way. Tom pretended like he hadn't noticed when she came out.

For about a year, Tom had had five of his paintings displayed at a local bar, with price tags dangling from their frames. The price tags and the art went mostly ignored. Tom promised a cut to Paul, the bar owner, if he ever sold anything, but so far, he hadn't had any luck.

To be fair, it was a strange place to masquerade as an art gallery. Half of the bar was built during Prohibition. Hundreds of liquor bottles were stacked up on shelves against the dark polished wood and giant mirror stretching across the wall. Women's faces were carved into the wood and shone beautiful brown in the dim light. The other side of the room was a 1970s addition with booths and orange tabletops surrounded by sports banners and florescent beer signs.

Tom's artwork in the corner only added to the schizophrenic décor. The biggest and most expensive picture on the wall, oddly enough, was a ten-foot-tall angel of death, crouched below the fluorescent lights. Tom called it "A Vision of What's to Come." Claudia didn't like it. In fact, she thought it was a cliché with the skeletal face half hidden behind the black fabric and slice of silver metal. But there was something in its eyes that was warm and inviting in Tom's picture. The eyes glowed a soft burnt orange like a fireplace at Christmas time.

It was odd art for a dive bar, but Tom said it was appropriate considering that the booze would probably kill you if you drank enough on a regular basis.

When they stepped inside the 1970s part of the bar, they got a jolt unrelated to Red Bull and vodka. There sitting at a red Formica table under the angel of death was Dan Johnson with his hands folded over his checkbook, next to a row of empty, brown bottles.

"Hello, Tom," he said. "I didn't know you were an artist."

The muscle lining Tom's jawbone tightened.

"What do you want?" he asked.

"A friendly drink and a chance to explain a few things," Dan said, sitting back in his chair. "Can I buy you two lovebirds a beer?

"I am genuinely interested in the art, by the way. It's no lie."

"We're not lovebirds," Claudia said, crossing her arms.

"Love is a complicated thing," Dan said, taking a swig out of the last dregs of his Miller. He started to peel the label off the side of the bottle.

She stared at him and imagined his face on a domestic violence poster as the victim, swollen blue skin circling his soft green eyes. Claudia used to think he was the abuser, but now she was not so sure.

He wore work clothes, a nice pair of dress pants, black, shiny shoes and a dress shirt with his sleeves rolled up. Maybe he was on his lunch break.

"I know you are angry about what happened, and I feel bad about it too, but I think it's time to put this behind us," Dan said. "Sara's in rehab. She's getting better."

"Rehab for what?" Claudia butted in.

"Meth," he said.

"Why are you telling me all this?" Tom said. "Do I look like I care?"

"I just wish you'd drop the charges against my wife," he said. "She used to be a good person, and I know she can be again. I really wish you could've known her before she started using. She used to be so kind, so normal, before her mom died."

Tom scoffed. "Too bad she tried to kill me. I'm not going to drop the charges, and I'm definitely not selling any art to you," Tom sputtered.

"I know it's hard to forgive, but please, think about it. She's doing so much better now that Steve's gone." Dan took a swig of his beer. "She used to come back from those support group meetings in such a good mood. The fucker was slipping her the damn pills. She didn't know what she was doing. You know I'm sure they fucked, too, in exchange. But I can't get that mad about that considering I've got a lot to make up for myself when it comes to being faithful..."

Claudia grimaced and crossed her arms, gripping her elbows.

"Did you have anything to do with that guy getting killed?" Tom asked, clenching his jaw tightly.

"Of course not," Dan said. "I'm not that kind of person. I do sometimes lose my temper, but there's a big difference between hitting someone and killing them."

"Oh, is there?" Tom said. "I wouldn't know. I don't usually go around beating people up."

"Please, just let me buy one of your paintings," Dan said, rubbing his face with his hands. "I'll pay you ten grand. I just want to make things right. You know how these things drag out."

"You know, I don't think we should be having this conversation," Tom said. He took a swig of his beer.

"Why not? Doesn't look like you're selling to anybody," Dan said loudly, motioning at the other paintings.

"Did you know they are evicting us from the apartment?" he added.

"It's about time," Claudia said, but she couldn't help but swallow. Her face flushed red out of nervousness.

Tom was calm and sat dead still in his seat.

"I have standards for where my art goes," he said. "I don't want it getting knocked down all the time."

"I'm sure the judge would find this whole conversation very interesting," Claudia said, suddenly. "Bribery doesn't go over too well, usually."

With that, Dan stood up, slammed his empty bottle down on the table and left. He forgot his checkbook on the tabletop, but neither of them were willing to touch it.

The heavy, wooden door slammed as they left. The checkbook sat there on the tabletop, the corners slightly upturned, next to the smiling Angel of Death.

Three days later, the movers came. From their window, Tom and Claudia watched them pull out the pieces of the Johnsons' life together – a Tiffany lamp with a broken stained-glass shade, the leather couch complete with slash marks leaking white stuffing, a desk missing one of its legs, and boxes and boxes hiding other violent secrets.

Down below, the movers reminded Claudia of draft horses with their stocky builds and rippling calves. They trampled up and down the stairs, stomping and leaping into the truck.

"Do you think he killed Steve?" she said. "He certainly had a motive."

"I can see it," Tom said. "Dan comes home and catches them in bed together. They argue in the hallway and as he's leaving, Dan smacks him across the head out in the cold with the shovel."

Tom stood up and joined Claudia back at the window. They watched the movers criss-cross over the grassy patch, trampling the blades. None of the movers had any idea a body was ever found there. It reminded Claudia of someone walking over a grave. It bothered her that they didn't know.

"It's all just speculation," she said. "Who knows what really happened? How would you ever prove it? Wouldn't Sara say something to the cops, if that were the case?"

"Not if she still really loved him deep down," Tom said, putting his hands on top of the windowsill. "Maybe they were even. Just think about it. If I really loved you, I'd do anything for you, lie to the cops, even kill for you. Wouldn't you do the same?"

If you loved me, you wouldn't lie to me, she thought. But Claudia said nothing.

She kept staring out the window. She had lost track of how many boxes they'd pulled out of the broken home. The pieces seemed endless.

"I don't want to ever end up like that," she said.

24 "GODDAMN TERRORISTS"

Kevin's grandfather didn't say anything when the men stumbled in and pushed Kevin down on the couch. He stared vacantly ahead with one hand on his walker, the walker he always refused to use. Sissies use walkers, he always said, but right now it had magically moved from back against the wall to his side. His cane was also close.

He looked shrunken and helpless. Kevin started to wonder if the man had had a stroke. Then he started to talk.

"My oh my, Molly," he said in a raspy voice. "I think I would like some lemon cake. Would you boys like some lemon cake? Molly, get them some cake, please." He continued to mumble.

"Grandpa, grandma's dead," Kevin said. "You know that. You ok?"

"I can't serve you boys cake without my glasses. I need to find my glasses." His grandfather stood up and pushed the walker slowly to his bedroom. "'Scuse me while I find my glasses. Secret recipe, lemon poppy seed cake."

Kevin sat up on the floral print couch and looked at the two men. He pushed his eyebrows together and stared but he didn't know them. One man looked vaguely familiar but he couldn't place it. The only thing really familiar about them was their rotting brown teeth. They were wiry and muscular, almost reptilian in how their muscles connected to their jaws underneath scaly skin.

"Angel's looking for you," the first man spat at him. "And when Angel is looking for someone, we're going to find 'em. It don't matter if it's LA or fucking Des Moines. Our people are everywhere."

"I told Angel I wouldn't talk," Kevin said. "I promised. I've kept my promise, I swear to God. I ain't a snitch."

"Let's ask Angel what to do with you, then. Let's see if Angel believes you." The man laughed.

Kevin felt abandoned. He could hear his grandfather rifling through drawers, pulling out boxes from his closet. He could hear him still talking in the other room.

"Where are my glasses, Molly," he could hear him shouting through the thin door. "Where did you put my glasses?"

Kevin swallowed down the sinking feeling eating the bottom of his stomach. What good is a seventy-nine-year-old drunk in a situation like this, he wondered. What could an old man possibly do? His grandfather was losing it.

"Please leave my grandpa out of this," he said softly.

He squinted his eyes shut and started to silently pray, while the second man called Angel on his cell phone.

"We found him," the man said. "What do you want us to do with him? Hmm. Ok... No problem."

"Who did you tell?" he said, after he hung up. The man gritted his brown teeth.

"No one," Kevin said, clutching the couch cushions with his fingers.

The second man pulled out a gun and pointed it at him.

"You told someone," he said.

"I swear to God," Kevin yelled, putting his hands in front of his face.

Then the door flew open and Kevin heard the shot and a yell.

"Goddamn terrorists!" His grandfather leveled the shotgun across his walker and took a second shot at the man with the gun. The other guy ran out the front door. Kevin's grandfather's hands shook as he reloaded and took aim at the man's ass. He fired another shot, but it missed and hit the van instead.

The shot man lay there bleeding on the mold green carpet, clutching the red spot on his chest and gasping.

"We've got to call the police," Kevin said.

"No shit, Sherlock," his grandfather said. "That's the first thing I did. They're on their way."

"Grandpa, I was worried about you there for a minute."

"Shame on you," his grandfather said. "You really don't know me all that well, do you? You know what they used to call me in the military, kid?"

"No."

"They used to call me the fox," he said, clenching his shaking fingers into a tight fist. "I'm an old fox now, but I'm still a damn fox."

Stan was leaning on his elbows and rubbing his temples behind the piles of paper on his desk, waiting for the phone call to come. When the call came, it was long distance and Sgt. Johansen from St. Paul sounded irritated.

"I've got an old man here who nearly killed a guy, today. We're waiting on charges. He says his grandson wants to talk about a murder in Chicago."

"He better talk or I'll shoot him, too!" the old man yelled in the background. "I recognized the goddamn gangbanging terrorist from the TV, and they threatened my grandson!"

"Let me know what you find out," Stan said and hung up the phone.

He cradled his phone against his ear and called Kevin's mother.

"Janice, we found your son," he said stiffly in a voicemail. "He and his grandfather are being questioned in St. Paul, after an attempted murder. Please call me back as soon as possible."

25 A PICTURE ON A BULLETIN BOARD

Claudia taped the flier with Kevin's picture up on bulletin board at the police station. She waited for the receptionist to get off the phone, asked to speak with Stan and sat down in an orange, plastic seat.

She stared at a mix of bricks and glass panels, and shifted her weight uncomfortably. The room stank of bleach but somehow it still seemed dirty. The '70s architecture was mostly to blame, combined with the rattle and hum of a decrepit air conditioning system. But it could also have a little to do with the people, unwashed and tired, sighing and huffing.

A man in sweatpants slouched next to her, with his head hanging back and mouth open. A grandmother across from them read a stack of community fliers through smudged glasses.

Then there was the parade of people coming in and pleading with the receptionist to get back their impounded cars, nervously thumbing through wallets and purses looking for proof of insurance and documentation to prove the car was really theirs.

"Yes, the car title is under my boyfriend's name. What do you mean he needs to be here to pick the car up himself? He can't get off work."

Stan buzzed Claudia in as the latest lady started yelling into her cell phone. The receptionist pointed at the notice on the wall behind her and coughed ahem, loudly.

"Cell phone use in the lobby is forbidden," she said.

"What are you gonna do? Arrest me?" the lady said.

"Yes, ma'am," the receptionist said. "If that's what you want."

The lady slapped her cell phone shut.

Stan took Claudia to a small room with dingy gray paint and a pile of cords hanging out of the wall. They sat at a small table and he sipped on his gas station Styrofoam cupful of coffee.

"I haven't heard from Janice so I'm guessing there's nothing new with Kevin," she said. "But since I'm here, I might as well ask."

"Well, I do have news," Stan said. He reached forward across the table and pulled the fliers out of Claudia's hands. He tossed them in the wastebasket with a heavy thunk. "No need for these anymore.

"You can stop walking up and down the street handing out fliers. We believe we know where he is. He's staying with a relative in Minnesota."

"Janice knows this?" she said.

"She's been informed of his whereabouts."

"Thank God he's all right," Claudia said.

"There's more to it, isn't there?" she said. "I like to think of you as my friend, Stan." Claudia leaned her elbows on the table. "You can tell me."

"I know," he said. "But it's not all good news. It might have been better for the boy if we hadn't found him."

"What do you mean?"

"It's just a matter of time before we extradite him across state lines on murder charges."

"Seriously?"

"Seriously."

Stan had on a neutral expression, like a judge in a courtroom. His eyebrows and mouth formed straight lines across his face.

"But why would he do that?" she said. "Why would he kill that man, Stan? He's just a kid."

"You know, darling, I can't read minds," he said, shrugging. "He's not talking. I really shouldn't even be telling you this much, but a boy like that, running around with a gun, expelled out of school, you really surprised?" He lifted his palms up toward the ceiling. "We got a witness who says he confessed."

"But why? What was his motive?" Claudia's voice rose slightly.

"We think it was robbery," Stan said, sitting back and fiddling with his wedding band. "Less than 24 bucks in the victim's wallet. May have been gang-related."

"But that's so stupid. Why would anyone commit murder outside the place where they live?"

"Criminals aren't the brightest people, my dear," Stan said. "If they were, they wouldn't be criminals. They'd be able to find a better line of work."

And with that he swung open the door and walked her toward the exit. He buzzed her out, took a seat behind the glass counter and motioned to a lady sitting in the plastic seat in the lobby.

"Next," he said, sighing.

"So I guess that's it," Claudia told Tom when she got home. "Mystery solved."

Tom sat down and put his feet up on the coffee table.

"Are you supposed to be repeating that?" he said. "Isn't that a special secret with your buddy? Murder charges are usually not something you brag about before you've got them."

"He didn't tell me not to tell anyone," she said. She plopped down the couch next to him.

"Do you think Stan's playing me?" she said, sitting back. "Do you think he wants me to tell people that Kevin's a suspect so that the police can get the real suspect to relax?"

"Maybe we should just accept the good news. I think you're over-thinking it," Tom said. "Has Stan ever lied to you before?

This isn't some stupid CSI show. It's not that complicated. The police have the guy figured out. Now we wait for the law. We wait for them to arrest him, charge him, extradite him, take him to trial and for a jury to decide whether or not they got the right guy."

Claudia walked over to the window and stared out the dirty glass onto the street below.

"I know, I guess I just want to believe it wasn't Kevin. I don't know why, but I've seen him for so many years, since he was ten. I just don't want to believe it was him, you know?"

He was a different kid back then, she thought. She could still see him smiling and waving as he rode his bicycle out in the parking lot.

"Now we just have to wait for lady justice to decide," Tom said. "We both know she moves at a snail's pace."

26 A CRYING SHAME

Tom was at work and Claudia was deeply asleep on the couch when a loud knock on the door woke her up. She smoothed down her hair as she peeked out the peephole.

"Have you seen Janice?" Alice burst into the living room as soon as the door swung open. "I just, I feel kind of hurt by the way she's cut off all contact with me. I know she's mad and she has a right to be, but now, she's not answering the door when I stop by. She doesn't answer my calls."

"I know what you mean," Claudia yawned. "They found Kevin and she didn't even bother to tell me."

Alice nodded and leaned back against the couch. Her arms were crossed.

"It's such a relief they found him," she said, rubbing her eyes. "But after putting up hundreds of fliers, it's not nice of her not to talk to us. She was mad at me anyway. But I guess she has bigger problems."

"Yeah, like Kevin possibly being charged for murder."

Alice gasped. "Really? I hadn't heard that."

"It's sad, but it's such a relief knowing who it was," Claudia said. "I was even starting to wonder about Tom."

Alice laughed, but then went quiet.

"I just knew all along. I knew," she said. "It's such a

126

shame when a boy that young ruins his life and for what?"

"$24 dollars."

Alice breathed in. "Really?"

"I know he told you he wanted to repent for something but how do you know for sure it wasn't something else?" Claudia said. "What if he's innocent and his crime was watching a murder and doing nothing to stop it?"

Alice stared down at the coffee table and didn't answer.

"Just think. You see a murder and do nothing. You don't call the cops," Claudia said. "You don't step outside. You don't try to help the man, just leave him out in the snow. You'd feel pretty bad about that."

Alice's eyes narrowed. "That would be terrible."

"I know you'd like to think that." She shook her head. "And it speaks volumes about the kind of person you are, your kind, trusting nature, but the reality is that Kevin wasn't talking about not calling the cops. He was talking about something much worse."

Claudia thought back to the ten-year-old kid who first moved in. He was quiet and respectful when his head wasn't bowed down to a videogame screen.

"I've known Kevin for years," Claudia said. "And his mom. How does a sweet child like that turn into a monster?"

"I just don't know," Alice said.

27 TRYING TO FORGET

"Hi honey, how was your day?" Tom looked up from his laptop with a sarcastic smirk on his face. "How's the job hunt going?"

"I applied to three jobs today," she said, stretching out her arms and creak-cracking her wrists and elbows. Her elbow popped. "Christ, I sound like an old lady."

"You're such a whiner," Tom said. He took her arm and massaged it, kneading the muscles with his thumbs.

Time seemed to fly while she was applying for jobs. The leaves were turning outside. Tattered brown and orange-leaved branches bounced outside their window in the breeze and scraped noisily against the glass.

"Every time I look down, I still think of Steve Jackson," she said softly. "When will that stop?"

"Who knows," Tom said. "Eventually, you'll just stop thinking about it though. It will become a piece of trivia in your mind, like the spot where the Obamas had their first kiss."

"I don't know about that," she said. "Speaking of trivia, will you ever tell me what sparked your criminal record?"

"Still harping on that, huh? Will you still love me if I tell you?" he said. "Promise."

"Yes, I'll still love you," she said, nervously. Christ, she thought, what if he was a sex offender?

"You won't kick me out and change the locks?" he said. "People make mistakes, you know. That doesn't mean they don't deserve a second chance."

He joked but she could see there was a genuine fear flickering in his eyes. They sat down on the couch and she patted his arm.

"Tom, I'd be out on the street right now if it weren't for you. I kinda owe you."

He sighed. "Then just try to forget it. That's the best thing. I could just kill that cop."

He got up, went into his room and quietly shut the door.

As sad as it was, at least she knew it was Kevin who killed the man outside, she thought. At least she knew it wasn't Tom. She didn't need a cop to tell her that. He was her best friend, not a murderer.

28 THE WITNESS

Kevin couldn't help but play the scene out in his head over and over. The images just kept flickering back into his brain, as he sat at the table.

It was too simple, almost, like red paint spilled on a black and white photograph. The man's head was broken open in the middle of a snowstorm.

"I want to tell you about it," Kevin said out loud, interrupting the memory.

Across from him, Sgt. Johansen put down his pen and looked up from the form he was filling out.

"Excuse me?" the cop said. "What else do you want to tell me about?"

"The murder back home," Kevin said, shakily. He wasn't sure how much he should tell, if he should tell. What would happen to his mother?

"Look, I want to tell you everything. You just need to make sure my mom is safe, first. Can you do that?"

The cop crossed his arms and looked deep into Kevin's eyes. He was tall, heavily built, with thick arms.

"Oh, you're looking out for her, now? Sure, kid," he said. "I'm a patient man. But it's always a bad idea to wait to tell the police what you know. Usually, it's dangerous."

"I just want my mom here, then we can talk," Kevin said. "I don't even care about a lawyer, cause I didn't do nothing wrong."

"We have lots of time to talk," the sergeant said. "You and your grandpa will be here for a while. But are you sure you don't want to just tell me now?"

The snow fell slow and steady, in thick, heavy clumps, but it wasn't a white out and it wasn't icy cold. It wasn't the first time Kevin had left the window open after the boiler went berserk. The radiators kept him up at night with their hammering. It was like having a crew of roofers living in your bedroom, working 24-7.

At first, it didn't seem that weird, a person in black with a metal shovel scraping the sidewalk. But now, he wondered if he'd ever forget the image of that shovel scraping blood and brains across the ice.

From his window, he had seen the shovel hit the man's skull. He saw the whole thing over and over in his head.

The car's wheels spun and spat snow under the yellow glow of a street lamp. Caught in the light, heavy flakes danced down to the white ground. The victim got out of the car and waded through the knee-high snow in slow motion, swimming around his car.

A few blocks away, the train's bells ding-dinged. At the same moment, the figure dressed in black approached the stranded man, carrying a shovel over their shoulder.

The man reached down to pry a chunk of ice off of his car. Watching from the window, Kevin expected the person with the shovel to bend over and start digging beneath the tires. Instead, they raised the curved metal up high overhead and brought it down over the man's head with series of loud thwacks. He slumped over.

"You weren't supposed to talk." He could barely make out the words through the gap in the open window.

The killer kept on hitting the man's head, cracking it like a walnut, then turned and looked up at the window. Kevin got a good look at the face covered in a black mask, with gaping holes for eyes and its mouth.

The problem wasn't that he couldn't identify the killer. The problem was the killer could identify him.

He tried to tell himself that the thick snow kept him from being seen, but he couldn't stop the panic from rising up his throat and drying out his mouth.

The killer looked up at him standing in the window and raised a black-gloved finger, waved it back and forth and pressed it to a wide, gaping mouth.

He understood the message perfectly.

He knew there was no saving the man with his brains spilt on the sidewalk. Kevin had froze at his window and stared blankly as the hours passed and the snow slowly erased the red stains. He wanted to believe it was just a bad dream buried beneath a white blanket.

But the next day, he saw the killer in the hallway. He wondered how he could hide from a murderer nearly next door.

He cast his eyes to the floor that first time they crossed paths and examined the criss-crossed diamond pattern on the blue carpet – anything to avoid the steely eyed gaze.

"You're safe as long as you don't say anything."

The whispered words stuck in his head. They didn't need to be repeated. He kept staring at the floor.

"I ain't gonna say nothing." He looked up into the eyes of the killer. "Please believe me."

He didn't tell any of this to Sgt. Johansen, who sat there patiently waiting for him to open his mouth.

"Look, it was the blatantness of it that bugged me, that they did it so close to home, and they didn't care who saw, because they could deal with it," Kevin sputtered. "That was the attitude.

"They told me, you get in the way, we'll get you out of the way, just like Steve."

He remembered each word like a bad poem.

29 REJECTION

Tom came home and threw the canvas on the floor. The wood holding it together cracked.

"Rejected by another gallery," he fumed. "It's not the quality of the art anymore, it's who you know. Or maybe I just suck.

"What do you think of this piece?" he said.

Claudia took a good look. It was the face of a young woman looking over her shoulder. She was painted in various shades of red and looked lost in worry.

"She's beautiful," Claudia said, glancing up at him. "And frightening."

"Are you just saying that?" he said.

"Tom, don't be neurotic," she said. "You know your work better than some idiotic gallery owner."

Tom crossed his arms and paced across the room.

"You know what he said? He said it lacked depth or any true emotion, that it lacked a certain spark. You know the sad thing? He's right. There is always something missing from my work, some element, some kind of fire that's just missing."

"Tom, she's fine," Claudia said.

Tom stopped and stared down at her.

"Maybe I can fix it." He rubbed his chin.

"Hold on," he said. "Maybe she needs a little destruction."

Tom stormed into his bedroom and came back with a hammer. He held the canvas up on the dining table and took a swing. The back of the hammer tore through her eye, leaving a gaping hole. Another slash tore out part of her arm.

"Tom," Claudia said. "What are you doing?"

"What?" he said. "I'm working."

"You shouldn't listen to them, what do they know about your art?" She pulled the hammer away from his hand and placed it on the coffee table.

"Now, she looks totally twisted," Claudia said. "I liked her better before. I'm sorry."

"Do you think people will think I'm weird?" Tom said.

"Yes," Claudia said, holding his arm. "But that's part of your charm."

He sat down on the couch and she sat down next to him.

"You read the news online today?" she asked. "They decided not to charge Kevin. The cops say the kid's innocent, after all."

Tom sighed. "Great. That makes my day even better."

He compulsively clicked through the channels with the remote control and the green, glowing numbers climbed higher and higher in the corner of the screen. Faces flickered and snippets of words stuttered out of the TV like cut-off protests, "Be-to-sat-no-der-fine-she…"

"So now, we go back to you thinking maybe I did it, right?" He turned the TV off and stared at the black screen.

"No." Claudia said stepping in front of him. "I've never thought that and I'm sorry, Tom. I don't want to fight anymore. It seems like we're always fighting lately."

"You're never going to trust me until you know what happened," he said. "I'm getting tired."

"I know you didn't do it," she said. "But why don't you just tell me about your past? Is it that hard?"

Tom stood up and walked toward her, close enough that she could feel his breath on her face.

"What about my damn past?" he said. "Some people didn't

have nice childhoods with overprotective mothers. Some people didn't just have things handed to them. They had to take them. Some people don't like talking about bad times. Some people just want to forget."

"Sometimes, talking is the best way to forget," Claudia said. "You gotta let it go."

"Easy to say," Tom said. "You didn't live it."

"Why are you so suspicious of me?" Tom asked. "I never did anything that bad. Why not check other people out? What about Alice, maybe you should make sure her church isn't a cult? Maybe we should check up on that, go for a visit?"

"I know you've got a felony record," Claudia shouted. "Stan told me. You lied to me. And if it wasn't that bad, why are you so damn defensive, Tom?"

"You want to know about that, fine," he said. "I got busted for burglary. I'll tell you all about it, tonight. And then we can go our separate ways. It's your lucky day. Tomorrow, I'll even move out."

"Oh, burglary's not that bad, huh?" Claudia sputtered. Her hands and words were shaking. "Why didn't you ever just tell me?"

"You know in prison, they let me teach a painting class to the other inmates. When we were done, the guards carefully counted the brushes and took them away."

"Why are you telling me this, Tom?"

"It doesn't matter what I say. You're never going to trust me again.

"I was just fighting the inevitable, I guess," he said. "I knew it would be a deal breaker. I'm late for work."

Tom slammed the remote onto the coffee table, went into his room, and came out in the black work pants and polo work shirt he hated.

"You'll never understand."

"Why don't you try me?" she said.

"Meet me at midnight downstairs," he said, as he walked out. "And leave your damn cell phone at home. I don't want you calling Stan every five minutes."

On the other side of the door, the keys jangled and locks clicked as he left.

She knew it was just a habit, just a normal everyday precaution but it felt like he was locking her up inside. My Tom, the jailer, she thought.

30 TRESPASSING ON GOD

Claudia could still see the tornado when she closed her eyes. It was like a black, blossoming plume of smoke being twisted between some god's angry fingers. She could still feel the thick raindrops wet her skin and the roar of the wind against her ears. She could still feel her mother tugging her arm back toward the basement.

It was midnight and she tapped her foot against the sunken parking lot pavement waiting for him. She had a choice, she thought. She didn't have to go. But it was like a game of chicken with Tom at this point. If she didn't go, he'd never tell her why he'd done the things he had. He'd just leave. Was she afraid? Why should she be? She lived with the guy. He could've butchered her in her sleep at any time.

She told herself the moment she got a job, she was moving. She was going to miss the bastard. The gate swung open with a hum and a creak and Tom rolled into the parking lot slowly.

"Get in the car," Tom said.

"We're going on a field trip," he said. "Just try to understand."

As he rounded the corner, the red toolbox in the backseat shifted and thudded against the car door with a chorus of metallic clinks.

"This is a bad idea," Claudia mumbled.

"Don't look so serious," Tom said, with a wink. "Will you be my accomplice tonight? Ok, ok, just promise me you aren't going to call your friend at the police station?"

He kept his dark eyes ahead. Shadows and yellow streetlight danced on his face as they snaked through the windy, old neighborhood streets.

"Accomplice?" she said slowly. "Accomplice for what?"

"I know it's hard to believe, but crime can be fun," he said. "As long as you aren't hurting anyone. It makes for a cheap date."

"I didn't sign up for crime. Wait, is that what this is now, a date?" she said, looking down at her tennis shoes and blue jeans.

"Not quite." He smirked. "Don't worry. You aren't underdressed. No ball gown required, but gloves would be nice. Put these on."

He parked about a block away from the old church and they walked slowly toward the naked brick back of the building. It looked exposed and crumbling compared to the grand columns it was hiding behind out front. Pieces of old wood with peeling paint were stacked against the dumpster.

"Crime number 1: Criminal trespassing," Tom whispered.

"Oh, so there's more than one?" Claudia said.

"That bastard promised not to tell you what I did," he said.

"Well, technically he didn't," she said.

"Lot of good that did me," he said, prying open the door with a crowbar. "Now I have to find a new roommate. Do you have any idea how hard it is to find an apartment with a criminal record? Most decent landlords run background checks. I'm lucky I even have a job. A felony's like a fucking curse. It's like they want you to stay a criminal for the rest of your life."

The rotten wood splintered easily under the metal and he swung the door open.

Tom turned on the flashlight and the light danced up cracked, gray walls and peeling plaster in a wide hallway. He handed her a face mask. She put it on for a moment, then pulled it down so it hung loose around her neck.

"Tom, why are we doing this?" she whispered.

"Kevin kind of confessed to Alice, right? What's that phrase? If your grandmother says she loves you, check it out."

"Your mother, Tom. If your mother says she loves you, check it out."

"Right, whatever. I just want to check Alice's story out tonight.

"But to be honest, this isn't the first time I've broken into an abandoned church," he whispered. The light from his flashlight danced around, searching the room. "I used to do it all the time. For the art of it."

"Oh, so you're into graffiti?" she sighed.

"I've never desecrated anything," he said, his face deadly serious. "I'm not a vandal."

Their footsteps crunched on the paint chips and plaster.

"Did you steal?" she asked.

"No, but I took stuff no one wanted, sometimes." Tom swung open a tall wooden door with a creak, but closed it when he saw a room stacked with old chairs in one corner and a cracked toilet in the other. "Nothing in here worth taking."

"Well, that would be stealing," she said. "So crime no. 2 is burglary, then?"

"Technically, yes, but in my own defense, in order to steal you have to take something that belongs to someone else, right? Well, most of the time, there was no one to steal from and they weren't taking care of it. If something is abandoned and nobody wants it, who's gonna get mad?"

"But there's just one problem, Tom."

"What?"

"This place isn't abandoned," Claudia said, gently grabbing his flashlight and looking down at the shoe prints dusting the cracked tile floor.

"True," he said. "Make sure I don't steal anything then.

"I'll give them a donation to cover the cost of the damage to the back door," Tom whispered. "Don't worry.

It's not like I didn't ask for permission to come in here."

"You asked but you didn't get it." Claudia rolled her eyes.

"How do I get you to see it like I do? Think of it this way, there are no borders. There is no citizenship. It's just land. It's just space. And we all move through it."

"Hmmm, convenient," she said. "I don't quite buy it."

"These stairs should take us to the top of the tower," he said.

Their shoes crunched on pieces of fallen plaster and the stairs creaked and groaned with each heavy step. Tom's foot broke through one of them.

"Watch out," he said. "The wood's rotten here."

"Isn't your friend trying to fix this place up?" He crinkled his nose and sniffed the moldy air. "She isn't doing a very good job."

"You're not helping much." Claudia pulled up her mask, held onto the wooden railing and climbed.

Tom walked behind her lighting the way, occasionally putting his hand against the small of her back to steady her on the stairs winding up and up.

"Let's check out the roof." He tapped the last door at the top of the stairs. "Ah, my skeleton keys should work on a prehistoric lock like this. Crime no. 3: possession of burglary tools."

"Why do you want to go to the roof?" she asked.

"For fun, obviously," he said. "I'm sure it has a beautiful view."

Claudia thought back to something Stan said about criminals being stupid otherwise they wouldn't be criminals. But Tom just seemed bored and crazy. Still, she had a sunken feeling in the pit of her usually law-abiding stomach, like the time she accidentally forgot to pay for a carton of milk in the school cafeteria. She knew she should go back.

She lingered in the doorway. She didn't even have a flashlight. Tom had the only one. Claudia looked down into the blackness where the stairs had disappeared. She told herself the stairs were still there, but it was hard to believe.

Claudia took one uneasy step down and her foot flopped in search of the surface. What am I doing here? She wondered. This is stupid.

"Claudia," Tom said. "You coming up?"

She walked into the top of the tower, held onto the edge and looked up at the wooden beams overhead, the empty metal rods missing their bells, then out across the treetops.

"You can see the Sears Tower and the lake from here," he said. "Just like I thought."

Claudia exhaled slowly. The lake looked like a great black blanket to the east, and the stars were lost in the yellow glow of the city. "It's beautiful," she said, simply.

The moon reflected on tops of trees like a silver haze across black shadows.

"I used to break into places like these and sketch them, paint them," Tom said. "I have this thing for the skeletons of great architecture, the decay of wealthier times, the broken things, the broken people, these old buildings hide. I'd close my eyes and try to imagine what they used to look like, try to imagine them new again in their old ways. I'd paint them like that.

"It was stupid really," Tom said. "I was young and stupid and it was a fun way to spend an evening with a crowbar and a blowtorch and a screwdriver prying the plywood off old buildings. After the police came to my house, my dad started asking questions and digging through my collection. When I told him what I had done, he laughed."

"What did he do when he found out?" Claudia shifted her weight from one foot to the other. It was starting to get cold.

"He told me they weren't any good and he burned them, dozens of paintings and sketches, burned them all in the backyard in a big pit. You should have seen the pile of canvasses with their bleeding paints, curling and warping turning to black ash, spitting and popping chemicals.

"He said he was doing me a favor. If the police found them, they'd know just how many places I'd broken into. But he was a fucking liar. It was all for nothing. He did it cause he

141

hated me. Some of those buildings have been demolished."

Tom had tears in his eyes as he leaned against the railing. "I lost it and broke his jaw with my fist. Add assault to the list. I was 18, so I got a criminal record out of it, but nothing else. Nobody ever expected me to go to college. They weren't surprised when I went to prison."

"I'm surprised you went to prison," she said.

"You aren't afraid of me," he asked. "You don't think I killed Steve Jackson?"

"No. Never thought so," she said.

"Why do you trust me so much?" he said. "I'm sorry I didn't tell you about this earlier. I'll understand if you don't want to be roommates anymore."

"Tom," she said. "You don't have to move out. Just promise me this is the last time you'll do this."

"You look like a princess high up in her tower," Tom said softly walking toward her. The wooden planks beneath him creaked. "Maybe I should paint you like this."

"Why would you want to paint me?" she said, stepping back uneasily.

"I'm always painting you," he said, putting a hand on her waist. "You just never see it."

"I've always wanted to ask you to pose for me," he said. "But I didn't think you'd let me."

"I'd let you," she said.

"What else would you let me do?" he said, and before she knew it, he was kissing her.

For a split second, she raised her hand to push him away, but he grabbed it and held it against his chest. Why not? Claudia thought.

The smell of his aftershave mingled with sweet sweat and the warmth radiating off his skin. She was dizzy up at the top of the tower.

"Tom," she mumbled. "I don't want to ruin our friendship."

Before he could answer, they heard voices at the bottom of the stairs. "Shit," he said. "It's the police."

31 DEMONS IN THE DARK

Her first impulse was to run down the steps, but she looked down into the darkness and remembered the broken step. That was the one thing that stopped her. Suddenly, a yellow glow appeared below in the hallway.

It was just a light bulb swinging from the cracked ceiling. So Tom and Claudia stayed where they were on the stairs, listening and waiting.

"I hope they don't have dogs," he whispered.

"I don't know why I let you get me into this," she said.

But the voices faded and the light flipped back off into the dark.

"Angel will be here any minute," the man said, his voice barely audible. "Let's wait for Angel, have a smoke."

"Is that smart?" another male voice said more loudly. "Jesus. Let's step outside, at least. We don't want all our work going up in flames."

"Who else would be here at 1 a.m.?" Tom said. "Didn't they notice the broken lock? They can't be working this late at night."

"Angel," Claudia gasped. "The cops think he's involved in Steve's murder."

The two of them creaked slowly down the stairs, searching

for the broken step gingerly before planting a foot on each board.

"There's got to be another way out of here," Tom said.

They got down to ground level and could smell the cigarettes burning outside. Tom hunched down and peeked out of a broken part of the door and stared at them.

Claudia's fingers searched out the door into the sanctuary, running over the wooden panels, until she found a thick iron handle and swung it open with a painful creak.

Tom slipped past the door behind her and slowly guided it back closed behind him. Another painful creak that made her hold her breath.

For a moment, she forgot the men outside the door and the fact that she didn't belong here, inside the house of God at 1 a.m. She was struck dumb by the sight around her.

Above them, moonlight filtered through the cracked and colored glass of a dome. Streetlights flooded through the high stained-glass windows, turning the panes a glowing yellow and the Virgin Mary orange. And at the altar, a wooden pulpit carved with vines and small figures in the shadows, were all bathed in orange light.

"Christ, it looks like one of your paintings," she said.

Tom walked from stained-glass window to window but they were all darkened and boarded up at street level. He ran to the front entrance and shook the doors but stopped when he heard the chains rattle on the outside. They slumped down next to the doors and waited for their eyes to adjust to the shadows and the yellow, orange glow.

Their other senses start to sharpen. Claudia heard Tom's loud breaths, heard the men talking softly outside. Every sound, every whisper, every step seemed to echo a hundred times louder than it should have. She sniffed the stale air.

"What's that smell?" she asked, pulling up her mask. "It smells like ammonia."

"They are dressed like painters, contractors," Tom whispered. "But they can't be working this time of night. Contractors aren't that dedicated."

"So why are they here?" she asked, looking at the pulpit. "For satanic rituals?"

They started walking down the aisle hand in hand between pews. Their feet crunched on the layers of dust and peeled paint and plaster covering tile mosaics. Cans of paint littered the floor and plastic tarps covered up hulking unknown shapes. The place made it easy to imagine monsters and demons. When they got to the pulpit, Tom halted and stared.

"Jesus Christ," he said. "It's just like I imagined it, dreamed it."

There was the carved, emaciated figure of Jesus Christ on the cross with his crown of thorns, blood dripping and below him, a pile of needles and debris. Behind him, was a torn red curtain. Tom pulled it back slowly.

"He felt like 'God was watching him.' Isn't that what the dead guy said in the hallway?" he said.

About a dozen propane tanks, big plastic containers and lab equipment were behind it, dimly lit under the broken stained glass dome above. Claudia's nostrils burned from the sting of chemicals.

"Jesus, it's a meth lab in a church for Christ's sake," Tom said, stepping backward.

"Kevin wrote something about running from Angel in his notebook." Claudia coughed. "I thought it was just song lyrics."

"We have to get out of here or we're dead," Tom said.

They walked back to the back door, opened it slowly, and Tom tugged her hand.

"I can still hear them. Let's try the stairs going down," he whispered. "Maybe there's another way out."

Tom couldn't see her nod. He pulled her hand behind him and softly closed the door with another painful creak. The sound was like a stab to the gut, Claudia thought. The fear was that sharp. Once they were in the basement, he pulled out his cell phone.

"Fuck, no signal down here," he said. He held the LCD screen out to illuminate his path.

Claudia inwardly cursed him for not trying it before. She kept reaching into her pockets, looking for the cell she had left at home.

"I shouldn't have listened to you," she mumbled.

The basement was flooded with about five inches of muddy, mucky water. Claudia could feel it saturate her tennis shoes and creep up the legs of her jeans.

All the windows were boarded up down there too. Tom reached up and pried at rotten pieces of plywood.

"Maybe we can turn on the flashlight then," she said.

"Maybe," he said. "But I don't want them to see the light."

He clicked the button and covered the top of the flashlight with his fingers, blocking half the light.

"Ugh, actually, I wish you hadn't done that," she said.

It was bad enough with the smell of mold and rotten wood. But to see the stuff floating and glistening on top of the water, the rainbow hued oil, the dead insect bodies, the unidentifiable muck, it made the skin under her heavy, wet denim pant legs itch.

A grand piano seemed anchored in the corner but the bench floated nearby. Pieces of old tables and chairs bobbed by. A small thing the size of a black gumball swam by. It had ears. It was a head. The rest of the rat was underwater.

Claudia caught glimpses from the flashlight, of the brick wall covered in a white flaky substance and the cobwebs burying the ceiling. "There's no way out of here," Tom whispered. "Other than the way we came in."

"This is like something out of my worst nightmares," she said, holding his arm.

"I told you some dreams come true," Tom said. "You didn't believe me."

He climbed on top of the piano and gave her a hand up.

"Do we wait or do we go?" she said. "What time is it?"

"Almost 2 a.m.," Tom said. "They must have gone inside by now. They can't still be smoking outside."

"Well, let's go then," she said. "I'd rather run than sit here and wait. What if they find us?"

On her way down, she slipped on the wet wood and hit a few of the piano keys.

"God, I hope they didn't hear that." She cringed.

They waded slowly through the basement. She felt something brush her leg, something moving.

"God, I hope that wasn't a rat," she gasped, trying not to scream.

"Do you want me to turn on the light and see?" Tom asked.

"No, I'd rather not know what it was," she said.

They walked up the stairs, pausing between the creaks and groans. Claudia tried not to hold Tom's hand so tight. She was sure she was leaving marks with her nails.

"Tom, what if they see us," she asked.

"I'll talk to them and you run and call the police," he said. "I shouldn't have gotten you into this."

"How were you supposed to know?" she said.

"I should've believed my dreams," he said. "I even showed you that painting and you didn't believe me."

"I believe you now," she whispered. "I can't leave you alone with them."

"You're a faster runner than most people," Tom lied. "Just get help."

"No come with me," she said through gritted teeth. She grabbed his hand. "I'm not leaving you with them."

He pressed his ear up against the door, then slowly swung it open. No one was there, but the light bulb hanging from the broken ceiling was still on.

As he opened the door, Claudia could feel something wet touch her leg, and dark muddy matted fur streaked past her. She gasped loudly, then they bolted.

The two men heard them and turned to look as Tom and Claudia ran by. Tom knocked over a pile of old chairs and wooden planks next to the dumpster. The debris clattered on the cement.

Looking back, Claudia was relieved only one of them was chasing after them, until she noticed the other bending down and unchaining something. It had a round, orange head built like a large pumpkin with jaws broken open in a jack-o-lantern smile. The man kicked the dog and yelled "Get 'em." It started running after them, growling and barking as they dashed down the street toward the old Nissan.

The dog started to nip behind her ankles with shark-like jaws and Claudia prayed loudly. "Oh God, oh God. Don't bite."

Just as it was about to sink the fangs into the flesh of her leg, Tom smashed a piece of wood down on top of its round skull and it went down without a whimper.

Claudia's tennis shoes skidded to a stop just past the car and she opened the door, fumbling with the keys.

Looking back, she noticed the man who had been chasing them lying on the ground with fragments of wood next to his head. Tom had used what he could get his hands on from the dumpster to ward off his attacker.

"Christ, did you kill him?" she asked, breathlessly.

"I don't know, and I don't care," Tom shouted. He tossed the piece of the wood to the ground and hopped in the passenger side.

The car tires squealed and the engine roared as Claudia hit the accelerator hard and ran about a dozen stop signs.

Her lungs hurt from running to the car. Claudia punched in 911 with shaky fingers. Dispatch connected her to Stan, who happened to be working that night.

"Stan, the old church, it's a meth lab," she wheezed, barely able to speak.

"Tell me something I don't know, darling." He laughed a bitter laugh. "Come to the station so we can chat for a while."

32 A PROBLEM WITH AUTHORITY

At the station, Tom was fuming red-faced and fidgeting with his right foot. His heel tapped the ground uneasily in a steady rhythm.

"Crooked, effing cops," he whispered. "Sit there and do nothing to warn innocent people then tell us to come in for questioning."

"Tom, you are hardly innocent," Claudia whispered back. "We just broke into a church. Was he supposed to warn us not to break into it?"

They hadn't gotten a chance to shower yet or change their clothes. They smelled and looked like they had each crawled out of a grave. Claudia shook her pant leg and clumps of mud fell out. Dark lines streaked across the denim, marking the water levels in the basement. But at least she had had time to wash the blood off the nick on her leg, thank God, and cover it with a bandage. She didn't want to imagine all the bacteria seeping into the gouge.

They were parked in a room with orange plastic chairs. Stan glared at them as he buzzed them in and took them to a back room.

"You may have just jeopardized the DEA's whole investigation," he said.

"I should arrest you both. I really should."

"But you won't," Tom said, sighing and leaning back.

"I won't," Stan said, clenching his teeth. "Because it would blow the whole thing. But if you fail to keep your mouths shut. The moment you say a word, is the minute I lock you up. In fact, I would advise you to take an extended vacation about now, stay away from our goddamn investigation."

"We can keep our mouths shut," Claudia said. "We can keep secrets. Who is Angel?"

"You tell me," Stan said gruffly. "What do you know about Angel?"

"The guys standing around smoking were talking about him, waiting for him," Tom said, drumming his fingers on the desk. "They looked like contractors, scamming the church, pretending to do work but instead squatting and manufacturing meth."

"Does Alice know about this?" Claudia said. "After all the work she's put into it?"

"It's a fucking lost cause, if you ask me," Tom said. "You saw that basement."

Stan sighed.

"Angel is the key to the whole thing," he said. "We were close, before you arrived. Now you might have scared all of 'em off.

"Can you keep quiet?" Stan said, leaning forward in his chair. "Look, sometimes these things have a way of escalating. A meth lab can spark murder, robbery, domestic violence, gun possession... One murder leads to another murder and so on and so on."

Tom nodded.

"It's like a flesh-eating disease." Stan muttered.

"You think Steve was trying to warn Alice about the meth lab and that's why he was killed?" Claudia asked. "Or is she a part of this?"

Stan didn't say anything.

"You still haven't questioned her about it?" she said.

"She's a suspect, too. Look, when you are dealing with

organized crime, you have to build a case and get as high up the food chain as you can," Stan said. "If we blow it now, they bolt. We get them on the obvious drug stuff but don't find the killer. We don't find the distribution network. And it's not enough to know who the killer is. You have to have rock solid proof. Even then, juries are fickle. I've seen more than a few murderers walk."

"And Kevin, what about him? You told me he was the prime suspect."

"Sometimes, a few lies are necessary to find the truth." Stan drummed his fingers on the table. "I'd be a bad cop if I went around telling everybody everything. It wouldn't do Kevin no good either. I just wish the kid would talk.

"At least the kid was smart enough to get the hell out of here," Stan said. "Why don't you?"

With that, he escorted them out the door and hit the buzzer into the lobby.

"I'd stay away from Alice for now," he said.

They walked back past the rows of black police cars and got into the rusted Nissan. The sun had started to rise, casting a bright, cheerful glow on the trees and old buildings as they drove past.

Claudia could think of nothing but hot water, but as soon as they got into the apartment, Tom bolted to the bathroom and jumped in the shower.

"You have the gall to go first," Claudia said, banging on the door. "What ever happened to ladies first?"

After a few minutes, she was surprised to discover the door was unlocked, and there he was wrapped in his towel from the waist down with white foam all over his face.

"What can I say? I'm faster than you are," he said. "Sorry."

"My skin is crawling and you have the audacity to shave right now," she said. "Seriously. Get out of my bathroom now."

"What? I'm not stopping you. Go ahead and just hop on in while I'm here. It would've been much more efficient if we just showered together in the first place."

"You are a dirty boy." She playfully pushed him out of the bathroom, her fingers on the skin of his chest. She let one of her hands slip and push against his hard abs.

After he was gone and she had closed the door, she paused at the sink and looked at her reflection.

Strangely, she didn't look like she'd been up all night and dragged through a muddy basement. Her greasy hair framed her face in waves and her eyes had a bright and energized look.

Tom had seen her at a lot worse, like when she had an allergic reaction to a piece of cantaloupe and her face and lips puffed up like a fish. He had driven her to the doctor and nursed her through a zebra lobster hives phase. It took three days and a pack of Benadryl to look human again.

As she let the hot water run across her, she lathered up with about a half a bottle of body wash. The soap stung the cut on her leg and she scratched off the Band Aid. It took five minutes just to get the mud out from under her nails. She rubbed her eyes and forehead over and over, hoping it would clear up her thoughts.

She had kissed Tom. What did she think of that? It seemed like a good thing. But it was kind of buried beneath the murderers and the meth lab at the moment.

Would those men be able to find them? Why did Stan really want them to leave town? Don't cops always tell you to stay where you are while they are investigating?

She kept scrubbing with the pink poof, behind her elbows, behind her knees, the cracks in between her toes until she started to feel clean again.

Tom was the only thing that made her feel safe right now, she realized.

She got out of the shower and darted to his room in her towel. He was pleasantly surprised when she climbed into bed, pressed her soft, moist breasts against his chest and wrapped a leg around his hip, pressing him as close as she could.

33 FOR EVERY SEASON, THERE IS A BODY

Claudia had no idea where to go.

The worry was interrupted by a comforting smell. He was cooking pancakes, eggs and hash browns out of a carton. For a second, she forgot all about his criminal record and crazy ideas about breaking into buildings and thought he was the perfect man. He was in his boxers and an apron. But then again, who needs perfection? There was nothing sexier than a man holding a spatula, she thought. She blushed slightly as she sat down at the kitchen table.

"Ahh, there's a reason I keep you around," she said, smiling, as he slid the eggs onto her plate. "Many, actually."

"We need a good meal before we hit the road," he said.

"Well, where are we going, exactly?" she said. "I don't want you to lose your job, too. Maybe we could just stay somewhere else in the city?"

"Finally move out? Take too long," Tom said. "And I don't have a ton of cash. I was thinking we could go camping, buy a cheap tent, make a vacation out of it, while we figure it out. I can get a discount from my work. It will be nice, just the two of us in the woods under the stars."

"Knowing our luck we'll be attacked by a bear or an axe murderer," she said, dropping a bit of egg yolk onto her shirt.

"Or an axe-wielding bear," Tom said dryly and handed her a napkin.

"Not funny." She wiped her shirt. "You have the weirdest sense of humor. I don't know that I'd feel safe in a tent after all this, even with you around."

"To be honest, I don't really care where we go, as long as I'm with you," he said in an overly syrupy voice.

"There's a problem though." He sat back in his chair. "What exactly are we going to hit the road in? Our car is pretty conspicuous with the rusted, flapping hood and we aren't that far away from that church. What if the same guys spot us on our way out?"

He leaned his elbows on the table and stared at her with those deep, dark eyes. She felt herself floating a bit, like she was on a slow-moving ship. So much had changed.

"At least they didn't get a good look at my face," she said. "All they got a good look at was my ass."

"It is a memorable ass, though," Tom said, laughing. "They might recognize it. But it was pretty dark last night. What else are we going to do?"

"I'll feel so much better when we're outta here," she said.

She furrowed her eyebrows and paced back and forth as she started to pack little odds and ends.

"Were you painting this morning?" she asked him, as she grabbed her pills out of a kitchen cabinet.

"I had to," he said. "I only managed to sleep for a few hours. I had one of those dreams. How did you know?"

"White shirt," she said. "I don't understand how you manage not to spill a drop of paint on it, and you spend most of your time around here shirtless, so why put on a shirt when you are painting?"

"I don't know," he laughed. "Did you want me to take it off? Are you complaining?"

He leaned over the kitchen table, resting his weight on his palms. She expected him to kiss her but he didn't.

She felt her face flush red. Here she was a grown woman and this man made her feel like a 12-year-old with a crush.

She started to pack a duffel bag on her bed. Seven pairs of panties, seven pairs of socks, three bras, one pair of jeans, one pair of shorts, no pajamas. Claudia always forgot the pajamas, but this time she left them on purpose.

She swung the bag over her shoulder.

Tom had all his stuff in a backpack.

"We're coming back. We won't be gone that long," he said, his eyes glancing toward his easel. He looked uneasy about leaving it.

"Tom, it's beautiful." she dropped the bag for a moment to take a closer look.

It was a woman in the clouds, surrounded by cherubs, wearing a golden halo and white folded wings. She stared at them intently with her blue eyes and a serene classical expression. Her long, blond hair flowed in loose waves.

"An angel," she said.

"It's weird," Tom said. "All this talk about Angel must have set it off. I get the feeling it's from the old church, but I didn't see anything like this on the ceiling."

"Maybe there used to be something like it at one point in time," she said, squeezing his hand.

"Oh, so you believe me now," he said, taking the duffel bag out off her shoulder and carrying it down the stairs in one hand.

"But you're wrong. That angel…" Claudia murmured softly as they wound down the steps. "I've seen her before.

"Christ, it's you." Claudia froze on the landing and gazed down at Alice. Her blue eyes sparkled. Her long blond hair cascaded down her shoulders in waves. Her skin was porcelain. Her mouth was upturned in a small, sweet, closed-mouthed smile.

Claudia slowly exhaled out the breath caught in her lungs. She wanted to be wrong, but she wasn't.

Alice raised the barrel of a gun level with Claudia's eyes. "Why don't we go back upstairs to your apartment?

A man stepped up behind her, the big, wiry one with no front teeth. He had the dog back on a chain again, slinking behind him. In the daylight, the dog looked like a sad stack of burnt ribs with liquid brown eyes. Claudia eyed the stocky skeletal frame and giant head coated with mud.

They backed up on the stairs. Claudia stumbled a little since she couldn't seem to take her eyes off the dog to look down at the steps.

Tom unlocked the front door and they walked back into the apartment, surrounded by paintings. Claudia winced and silently prayed Alice wouldn't look at the picture on the easel. She couldn't help but glance at it and then Tom. The Adam's apple in his throat convulsed in a swallow.

With the Johnsons gone next door and deaf Doris down below, there was no one there to hear them yell.

"You want anything to drink?" Claudia asked Alice. "A glass of water, beer, wine? I've also got milk and apple juice, if that's more your speed."

Tom laughed nervously.

"No thanks," Alice said. She sat down in the armchair and tapped her manicured, pink nails on the stained upholstery.

The pit bull sat on the carpet and waited with its mouth split open and tongue hanging out. Alice rubbed his filthy head and clipped ears with her left hand and held the gun in the other.

"He's good at catching rats. I've always hated rats," Alice said. She tilted her head toward the man with no front teeth. He grunted through an almost toothless smile.

"You know, Alice," Claudia swallowed. "Tom and I don't have a problem with it, what you're doing. In fact, I'm still dying for a job."

"Really," she said, smiling sweetly. "So you're good at keeping secrets then?"

"We are," Tom said quickly.

"Then, what the fuck is that?" Alice said, pointing to the painting. "Some kind of fucking joke? A fucking picture of an angel that looks just like me."

"I've always admired you," Tom said. "You're a beautiful woman. I couldn't help myself. I figured I'd give it to you as a gift. I didn't know."

"Yeah right, you didn't know it goes with my nickname." She glared at Tom. "It's not fucking funny."

But then Alice smiled and cocked her head to the side slightly.

"We don't need to give the police any ideas," she said in a cotton-candy voice. "The cops are so stupid. You know there was one drug bust I was at, they arrested everyone else but me. The racist fuckers think Angel is a Hispanic male. I'd like to keep it that way."

"Blond, blue eyed and busty," I can see how they'd get distracted," Tom said. "You look so sweet and innocent."

The man growled at Tom and Claudia took a good look at his scarred arms.

He kept scratching the pale, ashy skin of his face and shifting back and forth on his feet like a boxer. You could tell he used to be athletic, but the meat on him had been whittled down with each hit. The leftover muscles lined his arms and legs like white snakes stretched under too much skin.

"So what are we going to do with you two?" Alice said. "I know how chummy you are with the cops. I've seen you getting into their cars. What have you told them so far?"

"Not much," Tom said. "When you break into a building, you keep your mouth shut when you get caught."

"Is that what happened?" Alice said, with a sigh. She sat down on the couch, put her arms up on the cushions and put her black Jimmy Choo high heels up on the coffee table. "They caught you? It's not like my guys called them."

"An undercover unit saw us breaking out," Tom said. "Your guys are lucky they didn't spot them when we were running away."

For a moment, Claudia thought Alice might buy it. The corners of her mouth twitched into a small smile. She let her hand with the gun rest on a couch cushion and she leaned back her head and closed her eyes for a second.

"You know what?" Alice said, opening her large blue eyes. "I think you're full of shit."

She stood up, walked over to Tom, pointed the gun at his chest and slapped him hard on the face with her left hand.

"Dave," she said to the man in the corner. "You know what we do with people who talk."

With a wide, almost toothless grin on his face, the man pulled a roll of duct tape out of Alice's purse. He reminded Claudia of a child getting into his mother's belongings.

"You want me to beat them to death?"

"Not this time," Alice said. "I've got other ideas."

"Angel, just give me another hit and I'll do anything you want."

"After they're dead," she growled.

Tom leapt to his feet. "You aren't taking me anywhere or touching me with that tape."

"You just want me to shoot her now?" Alice said with a sweet smile. "I guess it's all the same in the end." She turned to her pale, ashy friend.

"But let's try to make it look like a suicide," she said softly. "She's been depressed for a while after that murder, terribly depressed and somehow convinced Tom to go with her into the great, glorious beyond.

"You know what they say, suicide is a permanent solution to a temporary problem," Alice added in a sugary sarcastic voice.

"You really think the cops will buy that?" Tom spat.

"Maybe or they'll just think it was kinky sex gone wrong. I'm not going to wait around to find out." Alice shrugged. "But I always find the trick to a good lie is to create one you can believe in."

The man punched Tom in the front of his head three times and he slumped forward unconscious.

Alice put her gun in her purse, pulled out a box of matches and started lighting candles. The boxer covered Tom's bleeding mouth with duct tape. Then he punched Claudia. She let her eyes close and chin hit her chest.

He covered her mouth. The panic rose in her throat and ended with the taste of adhesive on her lips. She tried to take slow breaths through her nose and hang like a rag doll.

The boxer dragged Tom's limp body to the bed and came back for Claudia. She let herself be carried. He tied their wrists together against the bedpost, like some kind of kinky, medieval torture ritual.

As he passed through the doorway, Claudia felt a moment of relief. At least he wasn't going to rape her, she thought.

But then she heard Alice's voice through the doorway. "I don't want anyone seeing that the piece-of-shit painting. Burn it."

Claudia's nostrils flared as she gasped in the faint smell of smoke. The room started to take on a haze. She guessed the living room carpet was burning, too.

She stared at Tom's face for a moment. He looked so peaceful with his eyes closed into curved slits. There were only faint red outlines of the bruises and swelling that hadn't had time to appear.

She blinked tears and smoke, then nuzzled her face against his chest, closed her eyes and smelled him. It calmed her for a moment. There were worse places to die.

But what would her mother think when she found out she died in bed with him, she wondered and started to squirm. Did she ever believe he was just her roommate anyway? Her mother always said they were going to get married. But she didn't really care what her mom thought anymore. To think she was creeped out by Tom keeping a hammer under the bed.

Now, she wished he had a knife under his pillow, a gun, a hatchet, anything she could use. Suddenly, she felt his muscles twitch and spasm as his upper body bolted up. He came to with a muffled gasp for air.

"The hammer," she screamed, but it only came out in a mumble.

Tom pulled at the ropes until their wrists were red and raw. Claudia stared into his eyes trying to get him to read her mind.

Finally, she shook her head and twisted her body until her

feet kicked against the headboard. Her body would have to be the hammer. One stomp, two stomps, three stomps, then the wood started to crack and creak. Tom had a harder time flexing his stiff body into position, but managed to angle his feet to the headboard as well, until they both pounded and kicked the headboard to pieces. Tom pulled the loop up over the top of the broken slat. They were still tied together, but free.

Claudia started to pull at the rope but Tom shook his head and pulled her, stumbling through the smoke to his desk where he cut them loose from each other with an X-Acto knife. They pawed the duct tape off their faces.

"Thank God for cheap IKEA shit," she started to say and he kissed her with the taste of adhesive lingering on their lips.

"To be honest," he said. "I've imagined you tied up in my bed before, but not quite like that."

They dropped down in search of air and crawled over the gritty wooden boards toward the window. The air was better down here and their eyes didn't sting as much.

"Tom, we're going to have to go out the window," she said, coughing. "You think we'll make it down three stories alive?"

"We don't have time to tie the bed sheets together," he said. "Fuck, there's nothing left to tie anything to."

They leaned out the window and yelled for help but didn't hear any sirens. The room was getting warmer against her back and Claudia couldn't stop coughing. The mattress was going up in intense yellow flames, burning fast and churning out heavy black smoke behind them.

"I'll hold it and you go first." Tom threw his comforter over the edge of the windowsill. "I'll lower you down as far as I can."

He leaned his body weight back. She held onto the fabric in an iron grip as she stepped over the windowsill.

"We can't wait," Tom said. "You have to jump."

"You have to drop feet first," he said. "You have to roll."

"What about you?" she hesitated.

"I'll try not to fall on you," he said.

He leaned and she dropped a few more inches. She dangled from the edge of the blanket, her fingers desperately clutching the fabric.

"I love you," he yelled.

And then she fell. It reminded her of jumping into a pool. She tried to relax but all her muscles tightened in anticipation of the ground. She rolled and rolled in the muddy crab grass.

She lay sprawled for a second and then heard a thud and a cry behind her. Funny, it was not the first time she'd heard something like that, she thought dreamily. It reminded her off the time she fell down the stairs as a small child, carrying her doll in her arms. The doll was almost as heavy as she was, with glass eyes that flipped open and a box inside her chest that made a crying noise if you shook her. Claudia had tumbled down the steps, hitting her tailbone hard, but the doll was the one who cried at the bottom of the stairs, not her. She was soundless.

And there she was, lying on the grass with the wind knocked out of her. Claudia couldn't speak. She wondered if her body looked the same from her window as Steve Jackson's did, minus the snow. Or if she looked like an old doll with blinking glass eyes.

When she finally managed to open her eyes, she saw a spray of sparks nearby where fireman were cutting into the side of the building. She saw big, black rubber boots stomping all around and the metal hinges jump upright on Tom's stretcher. It smelled like steaming water dashed against a campfire.

Then she was hoisted into another stretcher. Beneath the old tree, she saw Doris argue with a man with a notepad. She kept pulling the oxygen mask off and putting it on her dog's muzzle.

"You don't understand," she yelled over the noise of the engines and water pumps. "I don't care about the insurance money. My photographs, my belongings. After 80 years, they've become like little pieces of me. My things, they are who I am. I've lost everything."

"At least you're alive." The man patted her shoulder.

161

Tom was not moving. Claudia realized this as he was loaded into the ambulance. His eyes were closed. She reached over and tried to squeeze his hand. His wrist was wet and sticky.

She was in shock. She was in a collar of some kind, tied to a plastic board. She stared up at the building. She could see a huge hole into their apartment and the paintings burning. She could see the angel painting burning slowly, with a black wave of ash moving toward its face. Suddenly, she noticed pops of light.

"What are those flashes?" she said.

"Damn newspaper people," the paramedic said and loaded her into the ambulance. She expected a jolt but it was like floating.

34 PREYING

Alice streaked down the front stairs, with Dave behind her. She had met the man at a meeting two years before. It was one of the advantages of volunteer work with addicts – a steady stream of customers and employees.

The man and the dog had a lot in common, she thought. They were both strong, stupid and loyal. As they walked out the stairwell, she let the door slam in the dog's face, trapping him inside behind the glass. The mutt whimpered in the smoke.

"Sorry, buddy," she mumbled but didn't open the door.

Sometimes, it felt good to pretend she was a savior, to open the door, but Alice knew what she was, a predator. She liked the way Dave called her an angel. He was always following her around, like an unwanted dog looking for love. She told him she'd help him, if she could, but she needed a place to set up shop. She liked the way he thanked her each time she took away a little bit more of his life.

When Dave went into withdrawal, he had a tendency to call out for "Jesus Christ" over and over again. That was the spark that gave Alice the idea of squatting in the old church close by. The great thing was she actually got donations to do it and she got to play the hero. It made her laugh as she hit the sidewalk.

It was so easy to pretend. Alice was like a psychology experiment gone awry. She had read all the textbooks. She knew what signs people looked for to spot a lie. Don't fidget. Don't blink. Don't pause. Don't touch your face. And above all, don't ever look away.

She could already see the flames shooting out of the windows on the third floor.

Her neighbors were scurrying down the stairs. Many had pulled their shirts up over their mouths to block the smoke.

She put on her most concerned expression, tightened the edges of her mouth down into a frown and pretended to cry. Dave had already vanished into the crowd, but Mr. Washington was near enough to give her a pat on the back.

Perfect, she thought.

When the firemen came, she clapped her hands together at her chest, squeezed her eyes shut and appeared to pray quietly. But really, all she was doing was mumbling.

When she heard the neighbor next to her scream, she realized Claudia and Tom were not dead yet.

"They jumped!"

Alice started slowly walking away, back to the church, back to the beginning. It was time to collect the money and run. She didn't need to see if they were dead or alive. If they were dead, it didn't matter. If they were alive and able to talk, better to leave as soon as possible.

Standing mindlessly amid the hoses and streaks of water on the ground, Ted was busy talking to himself. He had gone down the list of names at least three times, counting the residents on his fingers, before the panic suddenly clenched up his muscles and crushed his fingers into tight fists. Why hadn't he remembered her earlier?

One resident was still unaccounted for.

"What apartment did she live in?" The firemen huddled around him.

With a shaking hand, Ted pointed to the second-story

window. The firemen ran up the back stairwell and pounded on the door.

"Is anyone there?" the rookie yelled and paused for a moment. "Coming in."

He kicked the bottom of the heavy door with his fire boot. The wood splintered but didn't give way. Then they started hacking at the door with their fire axes until the part of the door around the lock collapsed in and it swung open.

He ran through the gray air and his heart sped up as he saw the black woman lying in her bed, motionless. He scooped her up.

"Smoke inhalation," he yelled through his mask.

"I don't think so, buddy," his friend said, his boots crunched on the broken glass on the floor.

The rookie cradled her neck and head in his glove and carried her out running onto the lawn. His knees sank under seventy pounds of gear and the weight of her body.

"She needs oxygen," he said. "Why aren't you doing anything?" He shouted to the paramedics.

"Put her down, Jim," his friend said.

At that moment, he noticed two things: how stiff she was and that her black hair was stuck to his glove. The blood had congealed into a dark, hard syrup. He put her down on the stretcher and the paramedics shook their heads.

"Why aren't you doing anything?"

"She's been dead for a while," one of them said. "We'd better call the coroner."

"But she's still warm," he pleaded.

"From the fire, Jim." His friend patted his shoulder. "From the fire."

35 THE PRICE OF FAME

Fame could not have come at a worse time.

Not a single reporter knocked on the front door after Steve Jackson's body turned up. But the house of God turned drug house was big news, a freak show. It was unprecedented. And the fire was perfect for flocks of TV crews and news websites. The image of the burning angel made the front page of the local newspaper and went viral online.

It was visually stunning, and Doris told the newspaper people all about the mysterious artist who lived upstairs and saved his wife by lowering her down as far as he could. She told them he was on the brink of death after his fall.

What ever happened to fact checking? Claudia wondered.

The fact was, Tom didn't die. His right wrist broke and his left femur shattered, but he was very much alive.

"I may as well be dead," Tom groaned. "I can't even hold a paintbrush."

"It'll be OK." Claudia patted his arm. "You'll get better."

She stood next to his bedside.

"Why don't you sit," he said, tilting his head and eyeing the plastic seat next to him.

"I've broken my tail bone and I have a purple spot on my ass as big as a blueberry IHOP pancake," she said.

Tom laughed and his cell phone rang.

"Would you get that, babe?" he said. "I don't feel like talking right now. Tell Paul I'm fine."

"Tom's phone," she said. "No, he's not dead. He's just not answering right now. He's in a world of hurt, but he's alive.

"I'll tell him. I don't think he's in any condition right now to make business decisions and I don't think he'd want you selling his shit for him. Can't it wait a few goddamn days?"

She hung up the phone. "Some people."

"Apparently, because everyone keeps thinking you're dead, your work is going for a lot more than you were originally selling it for," she said. "Paul's hiking up the prices and he's getting a lot of questions from big-time curators. Some downtown gallery wants to do a 'Burnt' show of your pieces burnt in the fire, as well as the newspaper photographs."

Tom sat up a little more and smiled. "You mean they saved some of them? I feel better already. And it's not just the little pills I'm popping."

Just then they heard a knock and the young resident popped in with her clipboard.

"Sir, there's a policeman here who wants to talk to you," she said. "Are you up for it today?"

"Sure," Tom said. "But I am loopy on painkillers, so tell him not to trust me too much."

The resident pulled back the white curtain and her blond ponytail swished behind her as she walked out.

Stan walked in out of uniform. He had circles under his eyes.

"I'm sorry, Tom," he said, sitting down in the plastic chair next to the bedside. "You're just a chronic victim. It's the second time a woman has attempted to murder you – that I know of. I should've told you Alice was a serious, dangerous suspect. I underestimated her and I should've made sure we kept watch on you."

Tom glared at him. "You're a fucking crooked cop."

"I'm going to disregard that because you're on heavy painkillers." Stan glared back. "And I need your help."

His expression softened. He shifted in his seat and faced Claudia. "What happened?"

"Alice and this tall, wiry guy with busted-up teeth set the whole place on fire. Please tell me you already have them in custody."

Stan leaned back in his chair, crossed his arms and frowned.

"We're looking for them, darling," he said. "We're not finding them, but we are looking for them."

"Don't call me darling," she said. "You call me darling one more time and I swear to God I ..."

"You threatening a police officer?" he barked. "You're right though. I am a bit old fashioned about women."

"Maybe that's why you didn't take Alice seriously enough," she spat out.

Stan slumped in his chair. "I'm sorry. Tell you what, Claudia, I promise you I'll never call a woman dear or darling again unless I love her, unless she's my wife or daughter."

"I'll hold you to that."

"The sad thing is we have another victim." He sighed.

"Who?" Claudia asked.

"Sorry, you haven't heard?" Stan said. "Janice."

"How did this happen? How could you let this happen?" Claudia yelled. "You should've saved her."

"I'm not God. You act like it's my fault." He rubbed his eyes. "Maybe it is.

"We're trying to piece it together, but only one person can really tell you what really happened to Janice, and we're looking for her."

Stan ran his hand through his hair. Claudia noticed how a few silver wisps had started to streak through his black hair, lining the edges of his brow like the silver cracks on an old canvas.

"As far as Alice. Even if you think you know something you gotta prove it beyond a reasonable doubt. Juries are fickle. You'd be shocked by how many murderers just walk away. You know they've killed people. You can just feel it, and it doesn't matter."

36 A BAD DAY FOR JANICE

Janice had just flushed the toilet when the police had called to warn her that day. She had to wash her hands before she could pull the phone out of her pocket, but she knew it was bad news.

Her hands were still wet when she hit the buttons to call him back. But it went straight to voicemail.

She sat down to listen to his message. The policeman's voice was grainy and distant and she had to make out each cryptic word. He said they found him, but she could sense something was still wrong.

What if her boy were dead? It was a hard thing to think about, to wait to hear. She started to lurch slightly like a sick dog with a stomach full of yellow bile.

Alice touched her arm. "Are you OK?"

"I think so." Janice swallowed back the fear. "We don't need those anymore." She nodded her head toward the pile of 500 yellow fliers Alice had photocopied and brought over for her. The pages sat stacked under an empty coffee cup.

"Someone once told me when I was pregnant that having a child is kind of like having a piece of you break off and escape," Janice said. "You have no control over what it does, whether it's safe or not.

"You can't imagine the worry that comes with being a mother." She shook her finger in the air like she was scolding a remembered child. "That's what being a mother is. You worry they'll be hurt. You worry they'll fall. You worry all night when they don't come home."

"You have to have some faith," Alice said, patting her arm. "You have to believe that everything will be all right in the end. You have to believe in God. You have to believe they'll make the right decision."

Janice took a long, slow breath out and leaned her head back against the recliner.

"I know I've been angry at you," she said. "For what you said about Kevin. But I appreciate the help you've given me. You've been a comfort checking on me all the time. I hope he calls back soon. I'm dying to hear what he says."

"I am, too," Alice said. "And I'm sure it will be good news. Janice, you are looking a bit thin and worn out after all this. Have you eaten anything today?"

She closed her eyes and held on tight to the phone in her right hand. "I'm not hungry."

"You need to eat. I'm going to make you something."

Alice walked into the kitchen.

"I'm glad it's all over," Janice murmured. "Whatever it is. At least it's over."

Alice put the sandwich on a plate on Janice's lap.

"Please eat."

She went back to the kitchen and sliced up an apple with a large knife. The phone rang a cheesy electronic rendition of a pop song and Janice quickly answered. Alice set down the knife and came back into the living room, juggling the cut apple pieces in her hand.

"Kevin," Janice said. "Thank God! I'm so happy to hear your voice."

"He's OK," she shouted.

Alice had smiled. She liked to think she was lucky, but the fact of the matter was other people just had a bad streak of luck when she was around. Alice made sure of it.

Kevin was on a roll. She couldn't help but smirk when she thought of him. He had lost his father, witnessed a murder, two of her guys had been busy trying to take him out, and when he had called to warn his mother, well, as luck would have it she had been there waiting.

"Are you all right?" Janice asked, breathlessly. "Is everything actually OK there?"

"I'm ok, Ma, but can you call a lawyer? Grandpa and I have been involved in some shit."

"What shit?"

"Mom, you know we ain't supposed to talk about it on the phone at a police station. I don't have a lot of time. How're you doing?"

"I'm fine," Janice said reflexively. "God, I'm so happy you're alive! I could kill you."

"Mom, I need you to come to Minnesota for a while. Look, don't say anything to anybody about all this. Just come here."

"Don't you ever do anything like this again. Any problem and you just come to your mom. I don't care what it is. I'll always be here for you. We'll fix anything together. Just don't put me through this again. I can't take it."

She was making promises she couldn't keep, Alice thought. She could just barely make out some of Kevin's side of the conversation. Alice sat intently on the couch watching Janice's face for that moment of fear, that moment of registration when the information clicked together. It never came.

The conversation gave Alice time to think about her options. On the side table next to the couch stood a large vase full of half-dead roses and lilies. The water was a murky green. If that wasn't enough, the knife was also waiting on the kitchen countertop.

Janice's mouth quivered as she spoke and tears streamed down her face. Alice moved closer to the woman and put one arm around her. She patted her back.

She smiled a small, icy smile and spoke quietly to Janice.

"Is he cooperating with the police?" Alice said. "Is Kevin telling them everything they want to know?"

Janice nodded, and Alice's expression darkened.

"Mom, I haven't done anything wrong," Kevin said. "But I need a good lawyer before I tell the cops what happened. After all, grandpa did shoot a guy. It was self-defense. My time's up. I gotta go."

He hung up and Janice sat dazed for a moment, clutching her thoughts. Then she staggered to her feet to get a glass of water.

"Do you need anything?" she asked. Alice shook her head.

"I've never been so happy in my life," Janice breathed out. "He's OK."

Three seconds after she had turned and walked toward the kitchen a vase crashed against the back of her skull. It was like the power in her muscles just switched off. Janice sank to the ground.

Alice was left holding two large pieces of crystal in her hands. A few smaller shards shimmered on the linoleum floor under the florescent light.

She reached down and checked Janice's wrist for a pulse. She hadn't intended to kill her right away. It was so disappointing. But Kevin did have that kind of luck.

Most people took hours to kill, even with a couple bullets in them. Janice wasn't one of those people.

Alice dragged the body to the bedroom and lay Janice on the bed. She pulled the sheet up to her neck and closed the dead woman's eyes. She stood there, looking down for a moment at the sleeping corpse. Then she bent down and kissed Janice on the forehead.

"Sorry," she mumbled.

Death wasn't usually this neat and tidy. The prints on the glass shards didn't matter because Alice had filled the vase with water when she gave the dead woman the flowers. All she had to do was slip out quietly without anyone seeing her. With all the members in her crew, it wouldn't be hard to fake an alibi if needed. She looked down at the body and felt like an "angel of death" standing above it.

The nickname had followed her wherever she went. She

smiled thinking of it. The dead always reminded her of the first life she ever took. She was 14 years old. Her stepfather had rechristened her with his final words.

"Angel, Angel, why?"

37 IN SICKNESS AND IN RICHNESS

Claudia sat at the small desk in the hotel room, crammed between an armchair and a king size bed.

"Where are we supposed to go from here?" she peered out through a thin, white set of curtains into a parking lot below. "Where will we live?"

The Red Cross had given all of them vouchers to stay at the motel six miles away from where they once lived. Tom and Claudia had separate rooms, but she spent most of her time in his room, at his side, handing him a glass of water or helping him hobble to the bathroom on his crutches.

"This is effing humiliating," he said, staring down at the yellow frothy bubbles in the toilet bowl. "When did we get to the point in our relationship where it's OK for me to pee in front of you?"

He leaned on her as he washed his good hand, and she helped him back into bed.

She crawled in next to him and put her head on his chest. His wrist in the cast was close enough to her face that she wrinkled her nose at the smell of unwashed skin.

"Sorry," he said. "You don't have to do this."

"Yes, I do." Claudia breathed in the scent of his neck and felt calmer than she had in years.

"This is love," she said. "I'll take good care of you."

Tom kissed her hair. "In sickness and in health," he said.

"Well, the bloggers and news sites all say we're married so it must be true then."

"I don't remember taking any vows," he said, raising his eyebrows.

"You're right," she giggled. "I'd never marry you without numerous test drives first. What if I don't like the goods?"

"Well, you'll have to wait at least a few weeks before we can have a real honeymoon," he said, frowning. "I'm not exactly at my peak performance right now."

"Don't worry. I'll take good care of you until then," she kissed his chest down to his stomach and stared up at his beautiful dark eyes.

"Do you think we should ask the news sites for a correction about us being husband and wife?" she said, tickling the lines of his hips with her mouth.

"And ruin your reputation?" Tom groaned. "I'd rather just marry you."

She smiled as she looked up him.

A month had passed and Tom was still hobbling around. The physical damage had started to heal, but the anxiety hadn't. They were still not sure where they were going to live. Tom needed a place with good light and a space for painting, which meant every time Claudia liked a place he squinted at the windows and shook his head.

They checked out the listings and pictures online in the motel's business center and drove out to various places all over in different posh neighborhoods in the city.

The checks were coming in. Paul, now acting as Tom's agent, kept telling everyone Tom might never be able to paint well again after breaking his wrist and several fingers in the fall.

"He's a swindler," Tom said, laughing. "If I'm breathing, I'll always find a way to paint, even if I have to hold the damn brush with my mouth."

But the possibility had driven up the value of his surviving works. It also made Tom stare at his hand in its cast for moments at a time, anxious to grip his paintbrush again.

"I feel like I've been cursed," Tom said. "For a painter, what's worse than having your life's work wiped out by a fire?"

"You could have died, Tom," Claudia said.

"I know. But if my work survived, then I would have lived through my art," he said.

"But you'll make more," Claudia said. "It's going to liberate you to start over with four white walls all over again, in a new place, won't it?"

He frowned. She sat at the hotel room desk and held up the $30,000 check from the insurance company. "This certainly helps."

She put the check in the drawer along with a stack of papers that she had covered with writing. It was all she had, that and a small duffel bag. Claudia had never written much before. She never had much to say. But the claustrophobic atmosphere of the tiny hotel room had driven her to the desk in her spare moments when Tom was sleeping and she didn't want to disturb him with the TV.

"All those boxes I've been carrying around for years, all those stupid little trinkets and gifts I never really wanted – they're gone," she wrote. "We know what matters now."

The fire seemed to have cleansed them of all their sins. Claudia no longer cared that Tom had a criminal past. No one cared that they were living together anymore, whether they were dating or not. Even her mother had shut up on the subject.

"I'm just glad you're alive," her mom told her on the phone. "You want me to fly down?"

"No, that's ok, mom," she told her. "I've got Tom here."

38 IN PURGATORY

"Are you crazy?" Claudia asked Tom. "This is where you want to move? After what we've been through?"

She motioned out the window with one hand and put the other on her hip. "Look," she said, looking out the warped old glass pane. "I can see what's left of our old place from here."

Through the tree branches, she could just make out the brick structure in the distance, with its black, broken windows hollowed out like dead eyes buried behind scaffolding and plywood.

"It just feels wrong to move somewhere else," he said. "Like a betrayal."

"Tom, it's not like the money is just going to vanish tomorrow. You can spend it."

"If everyone runs, what's left?" Tom said. "And some of these new places have no soul. It's like the walls are made out of cardboard. All I want is a simple place with lots of light and open space and you there. That's all I want."

He grabbed Claudia's hand and squeezed it. "Look around."

Tom hobbled around loudly on the wooden floors. He ran his hands over the tall, white walls.

She liked the smell of the woodwork, like the smell of an

old library. She liked the way sun caught in streaks along the old wooden floorboards and the old, oversized windows looming along almost every wall. She liked looking through the streaked glass panes, glass that so many others had looked through before. Then she spotted the old radiators standing guard in every corner.

"Not even central heat?" she asked. "You're kidding."

"Nope," he said.

"I thought you were tired of all the banging," she said.

"Me tired of banging?" he laughed, pulling her closer. "Baby, I could use more of that."

The agent cleared her throat and crossed her arms. "With your budget, you really could do a lot better." She sulked.

"No, it's perfect," Tom said. "It feels like home."

They didn't have to hire movers to assemble the pieces of their lives back together. All they had were two duffel bags of clothes.

Claudia ordered furniture online and big, hulking men came and delivered it, carrying off Styrofoam and cardboard and plastic sheets.

So everything was brand new. It was eerie in a way, like living in a catalog, a place that wasn't real. Claudia missed the scuffmarks on top of the old dresser she had pulled out of an alley. Slowly, they assembled the brand new pieces and set a stage for their lives together playing house – a modern-style sleek, red couch, a glass coffee table. She always seemed to get stuck whenever she sank into one of the two overstuffed recliners.

Did it really matter what her couch looked like, she wondered. Tom was the most important fixture. The whole room changed when he walked in each morning.

They didn't have separate rooms anymore. But he did have his own space, the studio. Blank canvases were stacked against the wall, waiting for the touch that would bring them to life. No longer encased in a cast, Tom's weak, swollen fingers gripped his brush awkwardly. Despite all the promise, an uncertainty hung in the air.

Stan knocked on the door a few weeks after they moved in. His uniform was starting to look too tight across the middle. Gray stubble lined his jaw.

"I wasn't invited to the housewarming party?" he shrugged.

"How did you know we moved here?" Claudia said.

"Public sales records online." He shook his head. "If I know where you live, they might too."

Claudia heaved a heavy sigh and crossed her arms.

"I already called a few companies and asked them to remove your names from their websites. I've gotten a couple form-letter e-mails saying they have a first amendment right and it's public record, yadda, yadda, yadda, bullshit, bullshit, bullshit."

"Stan, when are you going to find Alice?" Claudia asked.

"We're looking, darl…" he cleared his throat. "No one's talking and that's making it hard. We've got some leads. Maybe we'll get lucky. We're trying."

39 IN THE MADHOUSE

Claudia knew it was a dream right away. Her mother was the one wearing the black robes and banging the gavel.

She looked around the courtroom and saw the whole cast of characters lined up in rows of wooden benches. A whole family of victims and witnesses tied together by murder, drugs and arson. It was like a funeral. It was like a wedding. There was darkness and there was celebration.

Mr. and Mrs. Johnson sat holding hands next to her on one side. On the other was Steve Jackson's mother and siblings wearing black and taking swigs of Miller High Life in champagne flutes.

Teary, bloodshot somber eyes mingled with giddy, flashing smiles full of sharpened teeth. They wanted justice.

Tom staggered up on his crutches and read the sheet of paper saying Alice was convicted of three counts of murder, two counts of attempted murder and assorted drug charges. When the sentence was read, Alice kept on smirking.

"You killed three people," Steve Jackson's mother screamed at her. "What do you have to say for yourself?"

"Three?" Alice laughed then opened wide her mouth and swallowed the tiny, frail woman. The skin on her cheeks stretched out in pale sheets snaked with blue veins as they expanded.

Claudia knew it was a dream, but she still woke up gasping with her mouth open. She held onto Tom tight but he didn't wake up. She tried to match her breathing to the steady rhythm of his. It took her a moment to remember where they were.

The room was pitch black like the hotel, but without the constant hum of a small, cheap refrigerator nearby. It was the new apartment.

She got up and tiptoed to the bathroom, closed the door and turned on the fluorescent light. As she buttoned her blouse, she looked up in the mirror and noticed how pale and washed out she looked.

Claudia quietly stepped out and took the train to a job interview downtown. But the dream hummed in the background of her mind as the train cars jostled down the tracks. Every time the doors swung open and shut, Claudia was looking at each new person, wondering who they were, if she could trust them, if they were her.

Would they ever catch Alice? Claudia wondered. It was like she had vanished in plain sight. She couldn't make up her mind which name to call her, Angel or Alice. Even the police weren't sure which name came first or if either were ever her real name.

Claudia got off the train, walked down rickety wooden steps and scampered toward the black office tower like an ant under the skyscrapers.

She couldn't seem to forget. Every time she walked through a crowd, she searched for Angel's face.

She kept hunting for her. Her mind could never rest. She kept finding pieces, fragments of the killer everywhere around her. Claudia would catch blond streaks of hair swishing off someone's shoulder. In the revolving glass doors, she'd spot a pair of brilliant blue eyes. Someone else would be wearing the same black pencil skirt in the crowd. Her mind assembled the pieces together until she felt her presence, until she could've sworn she was standing behind her. Claudia always wanted to turn and look, but she knew it was crazy.

Why would she come after her now? What good would it

do? She had to let go of the fear. She would tell herself this silently while sitting in a bathroom stall, with her hands at her temples, pushing back her hair.

She just knew somewhere else Alice was setting up shop. Somewhere else, she was smiling and charming her way into hearts and minds and poisoning others. She was busy asking people if they had given themselves to Jesus and trying to steal their souls.

40 DIVINE LOVE, DIVINE DEATH

"All you really need is divine love," Alice said, with a smile, to the nervous teen in the lobby. "Would you like to give it a try?"

She put the dime bag in the girl's hand and closed her hand over hers for a moment, before the receptionist reappeared.

"Let me know if you ever need anything else, Tanja. Maybe a job hooking up your friends?" she said, squeezing the girl's hand. "I'm happy to help you."

It wasn't the kind of outreach the resource center had in mind. Alice had just started her new job at a nonprofit helping keep youth off the street in St. Louis. She was going by a new name now, too.

She spilled a bit of coffee as she sat the mug down on the desk. She wiped it of with a Kleenex and sat down to read her e-mails.

She was sorting through the Google alerts about Tom and Claudia, clicking on the headlines about his latest art show and smiling to herself. It would be so easy for her to find them. She had people who could take care of them for her, but what was the fun in that?

When her boss walked by, she switched to an Excel accounting sheet that showed all of the nonprofit's accounts.

It's so easy, she thought, so very easy to keep tabs on people and money these days. Her boss paused and gave her a funny look.

"It's nice to see someone in accounting who seems to enjoy it," the lady said. "You're always smiling."

Alice felt relieved that morning. Starting a new branch of the business was always better without witnesses and she had made some changes for the better. So many people knew her face she felt she had to. It didn't seem to matter that much here, but it was still good to take precautions.

She'd straightened her hair into a bob and taken on a new name. Her eyebrows were waxed into thin, arched lines that hung over a new pair of glasses. She stopped wearing contacts. She missed the feeling of power she got from a higher vantage point, but she was two inches shorter without heels. Strangely enough, her whole posture seemed to change in flats. Her spine was no longer proudly arched. Her shoulders rounded forward meekly. But she wasn't a meek woman.

The night before she had disposed of a few things, including the white van. She and Dave had parked it up high on the bluffs near the river, wiped it out and sat in it one last time.

"The difference is amazing," Dave had told her, touching her hair with his latex-gloved hand. "Still sexy, though."

Alice had laughed. They had sat in the back of the van and he had tried to kiss her. She had pushed him away.

"Do you have any white cross for me?" He had asked. "I can always count on you to help me."

She smiled and handed him a plastic bag.

"You're an Angel," he said.

"Divine love, baby, it's all you need," she said.

Alice did have a marketing degree and the idea of a brand name had always appealed to her. It never caught on, but it was an inside joke that made both of them smile. She didn't like the obvious look of Dave's brown, rotting teeth.

"You're not having any?" he said.

"Never do," she said. "I prefer to sit back and watch. I've

dedicated my whole life to helping drug addicts feel better." She smirked.

She looked away as Dave pulled out his needle and spoon and slumped back in his car seat. He started yawning almost immediately and closing his eyes and his breath slowed down.

"When I was younger, I used to wonder, how come you never hear about female serial killers?" Alice mused, with her arm around him and her head on his shoulder. "It's cause we never get caught. We don't fit the profile."

She leaned over and held down his tattooed arms as he struggled to breathe. Each breath was a gasp. It was difficult to make out the blurred patterns on his purplish-red skin anymore.

"Sorry, honey," she said. "It's just, well, that face is hard to forget. It's one of the things I love about you, but it's damn inconvenient when you are trying to start over."

Dave's arms flopped as he tried to get up one last time, then fell loose at his sides. His unconscious eyes were open but no longer blinking. The pale skin on his nostrils was already starting to turn a purplish blue, the same hue as his lips.

"God, I love prescription barbiturates. Don't be mad at me, Dave. It's your own special goodbye blend. I've been poisoning you a long time, and you've always thanked me for it."

It had taken her just a few tries on other people to get the ingredients just right. The ones who lived hadn't complained. They just said it relaxed them. He was just going to drift off into a deep, breathless sleep.

She leaned over and kissed him on the forehead. He wasn't as pretty anymore as he had once been. His deep brown eyes had sunken into his face. His cheekbones were harsh and angular under his pale, blue-tinted skin. It was like their years together had been decades.

"I'll miss you, and don't worry." she whispered. "Jesus is waiting."

She slammed the back door and reached inside the front driver's side to take off the parking brake. The van started to roll back slowly into the river as she got onto her bicycle and pedaled away.

She didn't need to hear the sound of crashing water. Somehow everything always seemed to go her way. She had brains. Dave didn't have any left between the pounding of drugs and fists. It was that simple, she thought.

Stan stood at the top of the bluff looking down at the van stuck in the muddy riverbank. The forensic investigators and emergency personnel scrambled to pull the vehicle away from the rush of water with a web of cables and machinery wrapped around trees. The body was already pulled out and lay on a stretcher under a white sheet. Three guys dressed in black and yellow jackets were pushing it slowly uphill. A path through the thin trees showed where the van had plowed downhill.

The victim's brother was at the entrance to the parking lot, mumbling to himself with a dazed look on his pale face. Stan had told him not to come past the police tape, but the thin, gaunt man kept creeping up.

"Sir, can I ask you some questions," Stan said. It was more of a demand.

"I just want to see if it's really him," the man said. "I want to see him."

"You have to wait for the coroner," Stan said.

Stan didn't look forward to seeing the body again. It didn't look like a man. Like a dead fish, it was purple and soggy with whitewashed eyes after a few days in the riverbank. But the fact of the matter was it wasn't the bodies that bothered him as much as the crushed faces of the people who knew them. Nothing could hurt a dead man. A dead man was no longer weak, no longer suffering. But the pain of the living, that was hard not to feel.

"Sir, do you have any idea what might have happened?"

"No," he said.

"Do you know who he might have been with?"

"He had a girlfriend. You should ask her.

"They were going to move soon. He talked about starting a new life in St. Louis with her. He told me not to tell anyone where he was going, but I guess it don't matter now."

"Why wouldn't he want people to know where he was going?" Stan knew the answer, but the question would tell him something about the man's brother, how honest he was or how naive.

"I turned out all right, you know." He scratched the short brown hair on the back of his head uneasily. "I know it ain't glamorous working for a gas station, but I pay my bills. I got a daughter. My brother wasn't always, well, I know he did some things that he shouldn't have."

"Like what?"

"You should've seen him before the drugs. He used to love sports, had a shot at being a boxer." The brother's blood-shot, brown eyes wandered down the cliff through the trees. "But then it didn't seem to matter to him after the drugs, after he met her.

"That bitch was no good for him." His eyes narrowed at the corners as he fought tears. "You should talk to her. I probably shouldn't admit this to a cop, but I'll fucking kill her, if I see her."

"Who?"

"Angel."

"Is this her?" Stan asked.

It was one of the best black and white sketches of a suspect Stan had seen in his career. Her eyes were round, nose long and narrow, her lips full, her cheekbones high, eyebrows arched. Based on pictures of Tom's work, it looked just like her and still, no one came forward.

The dead man's brother nodded. And then another officer came to collect him. "Time to view the body."

Stan stayed there at the top of the bluff and looked down at the scene below. He could hear the man sobbing in the distance. He tried not to listen, but he could make some of the words out. "Davey, my baby brother."

Stan leaned up against a tree trunk and closed his eyes for a moment. The investigators were already squabbling over whether it was a suicide or accidental death, but he still had to let the FBI know about the connection. They were taking their sweet time catching up with her. He wished he were in charge of the investigation.

He knew that Alice liked to prey on addicts to build her business. Maybe she'd try to do it again. It was a slim and tedious lead to follow with countless phone calls to every nonprofit, rehab organization in St. Louis he could find online. If only the boy had talked sooner. If only someone would talk.

People didn't know how dangerous it was to keep their damn mouths shut.

41 THE SHOWDOWN

Tom was busy getting ready for his first show, "Burnt." He wanted to make sure he agreed with the curator's work arranging the art and photos before it opened, but the only time they allowed him to stop by was hours before the show, so it was not like there was time to change anything anyway. The organizers said they didn't want to bother him since he was in bad health.

"I hate that I have no control over anything," he said. "Damn hotshot photographer's in charge."

Claudia helped him hobble out of the car on his crutch and walk up the ramp to the museum. Inside, everything was painted white and brightly lit. The photos of his paintings had been blown up ten feet high and were in order of when they were shot. You could see the angel's face degrade, become covered in black soot and curl up and shrivel into nothing. At the end of the exhibit, there was a pile of the burnt canvasses surrounded by a velvet rope, intertwined with yellow police tape.

"Fucking joke." Tom hobbled over, ripped the police tape off and threw it in the black trashcan in the corner. "That's my contribution.

"I can't really take any credit for this." Tom sat down on

the bench, stared at the pile and sighed. "It's all the work of a freak accident, isn't it? Sure, the photographer did a great job capturing it, but still, did I ever have any real talent?"

She winced as she sat down next to him and her arm around him. It still hurt to sit, but she did it anyway to be near him.

"Of course, you have talent," she said. "Don't make me slap you. It was the photographer and the rest of us who got lucky. If it weren't for the freak accident, no one would have seen that painting other than a handful of people."

"The newspapers love it, don't they?" The gravelly voice behind them made both of them jump an inch off the bench.

Stan walked up dressed like a cop trying not to look like a cop in a pin-striped suit with boxy shoulders and crooked iron lines. Professional attire didn't seem to suit him as naturally as a uniform.

"What, are you my personal bodyguard now?" Tom said.

"No, but it wouldn't hurt to hire one." Stan's eyes scanned the room.

"It's nice to have the suspect's face capturing the public's interest." He nodded his head toward a ten-foot-tall photo of Alice's face curled up on a black and blue canvas. "It means I get a lotta anonymous calls. Somebody even thinks Angel is crazy enough to show up tonight. Most of these people are totally off their rocker though. One of 'em asked me to arrest their cat for stealing. But who knows? Maybe the cat did have a thing for shiny objects."

"You always say it's not your investigation," Claudia said. "Then why do you spend so much time talking to us?"

"It's really the FBI and DEA's investigation. And I don't like the way they're taking their sweet-ass time."

"I don't like the way you are taking your own sweet-ass time," Tom said. "I don't understand how you could have interviewed her after the murder on the corner and not known."

"It's not enough to know who did it anymore. You have to have overwhelming, indisputable proof," Stan said. "They call it the 'CSI effect.' The public expects us to have this amazing forensic evidence, DNA, blood specks, the smoking gun. But the fact is Alice almost always knows her victims. She gets to 'em. She's a serial killer who kills with simple tools. There's never a smoking gun. It's a clever pattern. She killed Dave with drugs, but the defense would call that a suicide. Your case is strong, but it's a fire she didn't even set. With the Jackson guy, it was a shovel. But there are no prints on it. If she had any bloody clothes in her apartment the fire cleaned 'em out.

"What about Janice?" Claudia said. "Wasn't there some evidence there that didn't get destroyed? Her apartment wasn't completely gutted like ours was."

"Alice used a crystal vase to kill her, but she's the one who gave her the flowers," Stan said. "So what would prints prove, even if we could find them in the middle of a fire scene?

"The only thing we've got is testimony from you two and the Kevin kid."

"You'd think that would be worth a lot," Tom said.

"It's worth a lot as long as the three of you are alive," Stan said.

"But she wouldn't try to take us out after all the publicity, would she?" Tom asked. "She's a drug dealer, not a psychopath."

"My guess is she's both," Stan said. "You know that saying, if you love what you do, you'll never work a day in your life?"

"Are you working tonight?" Claudia asked.

"Not technically," he said. "But I'm going to go brief security anyway. Good luck tonight." He turned and walked away.

"And here I am thinking he just showed up to buy some of my work," Tom said in a dry, sarcastic voice.

Claudia exhaled and stood up. She couldn't take sitting anymore. Tom slumped forward and watched as a group of men and women dressed in crisp white shirts and black bow ties entered the room pushing carts full of tiny circular pieces of meat and cheese topped with mysterious green tufts.

"Maybe now is not the time to be in the limelight." He sighed.

"What do you mean?" she asked. "You've waited your whole life for people to appreciate your art."

The women began stacking the clinking glasses in a pyramid on a white-table-cloth covered table near the end of the exhibit. Their heels made clop, clop sounds as they shifted and stacked the glasses. Claudia shifted uneasily on her feet and glanced over, almost expecting to see Alice.

"It's not my art," Tom said. "Maybe we should just go home. I don't belong here."

"Tom, you are the most talented person I know," she said. "I've believed in you from the start. You have to stay. You can't live your life in fear and give up what you've always wanted."

"Dude, they are dressed better than I am," he said, tugging at the collar of his spotless white shirt.

It was true, so she didn't say anything. She looked down at her brown, flowing dress, borrowed from a friend. The shoes were a little too big, but Claudia didn't care. Tom didn't feel like shopping on crutches and she didn't feel like leaving Tom.

The people, most dressed in black and white, started to trickle in. Tom kept sitting there like a part of the exhibit, a broken down, hobbling artist after the fire. Claudia helped him to his feet and guided him to a chair at the tall table in the corner and parked a glass of white wine in front of him. She took his crutch away and stacked it against the wall.

As she walked back, she noticed the curved, black sequined back of an elderly lady pushing a walker, with a slim woman in a simple, black dress holding her arm.

"My God, it's Doris!" Claudia said. "Hey, Doris. It's amazing to see you out of the house."

"This is my daughter," she said. "She came back to take care of me after the fire. Isn't it great? I'm not a shut-in anymore."

By the time Claudia got back to the table, Tom was smiling up at three beautiful women circling around him.

"It's shame we won't have the pleasure of seeing the original work. I know what she's done, but she looks so beautiful, so innocent. I'd love to pose for you."

The woman in the short, black satin dress bent forward as she shook Tom's left hand. It was like she had gift-wrapped all her best parts in the tight, shiny fabric. "I'm sure it's been very hard."

"Yes, it has," Tom said, keeping his eyes on hers.

Another woman in a black and white striped dress handed him her card. "I understand you're not actually married."

"No. My God." Tom said. "I know who you are. I've waited years to meet you. I love your work."

"You know, I can't help but notice that that cast is awfully boring," she said, touching his shoulder with a small delicate hand. "Maybe we can go somewhere private later and I can paint on it and maybe some other places, as well?"

Claudia's face drained of all color as she walked over there. She put her arm around Tom's neck and nuzzled her face into his ear.

"Flirting is fine, but I can't stand it when a woman touches my man," she whispered. "She touches you one more time like that, and I might just kill her."

He smiled and sighed. "I love you too, baby." She could smell scotch on his breath.

James, the photographer, arrived and started drinking with Tom. He was a tall, lanky man with glasses and a slouch in one shoulder where the strap usually cut in from his camera bag.

"I just like to sit here and observe the reactions to my work," he said, shrugging.

Claudia wondered if he was self conscious without being able to hide behind his lenses, if he felt as hollow as Tom about the dozens of people coming up to him and shaking his hand. But that didn't seem to be the case. He stood tall with his chest puffed out, in an exaggerated gesture of pride.

"Absolutely amazing work," a man spat out over the noise, into his ear. "How you were able to capture these kinds of images in those lighting conditions against the blaze of the fire is just amazing from a technical standpoint, as well as an artistic one."

"I know, I know." James smiled and ran his hand through his thinning hair.

Tom was slamming back the drinks now. He had moved past the glasses of wine and on to whiskey. He was spinning the little red straw, chasing the ice cubes in his glass and laughing to James.

"What does all this mean?" Tom slurred into the photographer's ear. "Is success in art just an accident? Is it just a matter of the right people saying your work is worth looking at? I guess I should thank you for getting their attention."

James just smiled slyly. He studied Tom for a moment and squinted to focus his eyes, after a few drinks of his own.

"My work is no accident," he said. "And neither is yours. Buddy, you gotta learn to sell yourself."

"I don't want to sell myself," Tom said, slapping his hand on the table.

"Tom, are you supposed to be drinking like this when you are taking painkillers?" Claudia asked. "Let me take you home."

She brought him his jacket and his crutch. It wasn't even that late, only 8 p.m. according to her watch. But Tom didn't need any more drinks.

He lurched forward from the table and leaned heavily on his crutch. She walked him to the steps and helped steady him as he lowered his leg down each step. He sat down on the bottom step with his bad leg stretched out in front of him like a stiff, overstuffed carnival prize.

"Wait and I'll pick you up," she said, walking briskly toward the parking lot. Her heels scraped against the cement in a steady rhythm. Her right shoe kept slipping off her heel. Claudia wanted to sprint but didn't want to twist her ankle.

She started her car and felt ashamed to be driving such a lowly vehicle to such a highbrow event. They should have rented something fancier or shown up in a limo. What kind of rising star in the art world comes to his show in an old, rusted Nissan?

As she rolled up to the front steps, she couldn't help but

curse. Tom was nowhere to be seen. She flicked on the hazard lights and waited. She wondered if he had snuck off with the woman in the satin dress. She looked for him in the dimming light.

But then she saw his shadowy silhouette hobbling on the other side of the road staring at something off in the distance.

She got out of the car to help Tom get into the passenger side.

"That SUV. I thought I saw her get in that SUV." He pointed down the street.

"You're drunk, Tom," Claudia said. "Get in the car."

"She looked different. Dark hair. Maybe I'm imagining it, but she walks like that."

Claudia instinctively reached into her pockets to grab her phone but her palms slid over the empty curves of the brown dress. She had been so busy gathering Tom's belongings and getting him out the door, she had forgotten her own coat with her phone in it. A nervous feeling sank into her stomach.

Before she had time to ask for his, she heard the roar of a large engine and saw the Chevy Suburban with black tinted windows accelerating down the street at about 80 mph straight at them. She darted up the stairs back toward the gallery. Tom hobbled as fast as he could but fell flat on his face against the steps. She ran back down and pulled him up as fast as she could. Her heels loudly scratched the cement.

All four wheels screeched and struggled to stay on the ground at the same time as the Suburban swerved toward them.

The SUV slammed into the Nissan, crunching it into a twisted hunk of metal coming right at them. It climbed most of the stairs, then stalled at the top, inches away from where Tom and Claudia crouched behind a pillar and screamed.

Alice stiffly lifted her head and stared at them. Her eyes were open wide with surprise. They all wondered how the hell she had missed. As she moved her arm to shift into reverse, little flecks of glass and drops of blood slipped off, like rubies and diamonds.

Two men watched from the sidewalk. One of them was taking video with his phone.

"Mother fucker," Claudia shouted as she pulled Tom to his feet. "Call the police."

"I'm right here," Stan hollered through his squad car's window. He leveled his shotgun at the SUV and shattered the windshield with his first shot.

Three stunned security guards poured out the front entrance with their weapons drawn.

The SUV had already rolled backward down the stairs, and unhinged the remains of the Nissan. Through a barrage of bullets, Alice put the Chevy into drive and accelerated on wobbly wheels back to fifty, sixty, seventy miles and hour with a smoking engine and one flat tire. Claudia stared at the tail end of the SUV as it accelerated down the street. It had a small, gray "Jesus Saves" bumper sticker.

Stan trailed Alice in his black, unmarked squad with lights flashing and siren blasting. He took three shots and watched as the SUV clipped a truck past the stoplight and spun around back and struck a utility pole. The wood snapped in half and the transformer on top fell to the ground with a bright yellow flash of light, then darkness.

He braked and swerved to miss the pole and hit the curb with a jolt that travelled up each vertebra in his spine. Stan staggered out of his police car and watched as the SUV caught fire. The transformer sat on top of the metal hood like a warning beacon.

Wild flames licked the metal, lapping quickly, as the ambulance pulled up. A fire engine's siren echoed in the distance.

She was twisting and turning in there. Even though she was a killer, it felt like a kind of murder to leave her trapped in a burning vehicle. Stan wanted to pull on the door handle, but he knew the skin on his hand would blister against the melting plastic and he could be electrocuted.

The door was crushed inward like an old aluminum can. The flames built up higher and devoured the dash and airbag, the seats and her. He had to step back from the hellish roar of heat.

Plumes of smoke rose into the sky, and the arms of the fire split out of the SUVs broken windows. The sun had already set with the last of its orange and red streaks spilt across the bottom of a dark sky. It looked like all that was left of the world, Stan thought. It looked like the whole world was on fire.

42 MAKING IT UP

Tom and Claudia stood staring at the remains of their car, a surreal hunk of metal outside an art exhibit. The hazard lights were blinking in the dark. The art exhibit attendees came outside and pointed at the wreck. Some still carried their wine glasses.

Claudia couldn't wait to get out of there. The EMTs had asked her and Tom if they wanted to go to the hospital a million times.

"Are you sure you are ok?" they had asked.

She held onto Tom's arm and said she thought she was. It was actually kind of hard to tell. There were pangs and bruises from the stairs that hadn't shown their colors yet. Tom reached into his pocket for his cell phone and found it had been smashed into pieces of black plastic.

"All I want to do is go home," she said to Tom.

"I just want another drink," he said.

Someone brought him a glass of champagne and he took a swig in front of the remains of the old car. He couldn't help but laugh.

"It's art now," he said. "What a way to go." He threw his glass at it and it shattered. "Why don't we sell this, too?"

"Don't litter," a nearby cop barked.

"What does it matter?" Tom shouted back. "It's a mess anyway."

Claudia laughed, too. She was relieved to be alive. "Come on," she said, pulling Tom up. "Let's get the hell out of here."

She walked in front of the line of people waiting for cabs and stuck out her hand. None of them said anything to her as they stepped into the cab. Tom's crutch was spread across the back. Neither of them wore their seat belts. There was no way fate would keep fucking with them like that, she thought.

They pulled up in front of their new building and climbed the old, creaky stairs.

While she was fumbling with her keys to open the wooden door, Claudia could hear the landline ringing on the other side over and over. No one important ever called on that line, just creditors robo-calling the wrong number.

After kicking off his shoe, Tom hobbled over and answered the phone. He put his crutch against the wall and leaned one hand against the bookcase for support.

"My agent," he whispered. "Yep. Sounds great. Thanks."

Claudia hung up his suit jacket for him in the closet and then wandered into the bedroom and took off her borrowed earrings. She threw a sparkly crystal necklace on top of the dresser.

She wandered into the bathroom and washed the makeup off her face with cold water until the black splotches of mascara beneath her eyes disappeared. She wiped the water droplets off her face with a soft, new towel. She pressed it against her closed eyes and tried not to think about the evening they had had. Instead, she took in a deep breath and smelled the scent of lavender detergent. She brushed her teeth and took out her blurry contacts. They were all automatic actions, things she did all the time, but they felt different. They felt heavier. The adrenaline had worn off.

"I'm rich and famous now," Tom staggered into the bedroom and lay down on the king-sized bed. "Do you love me more?"

Claudia followed him and let the dress drop onto the floor

199

into a puddle of brown fabric. She kicked off her heels, slipped under the sheets and put her arms around his wide shoulders. The heaviness floated away the instant she smelled his skin.

"You know I've always loved you," she said. She unbuttoned his shirt and slid her hands under the wrinkled cotton, touching his warm skin.

"That's news to me," he said, putting his good arm around her. "Why didn't you tell me before?"

She frowned and ran her fingers across his smooth jaw, turning his face towards hers.

"Tom, I swear, I have for a long time," her voice sounded scratched after all they'd been through. "It kind of scared me how much. It crept up on me a little bit more each day. And I'm sorry it took me so long to admit. But almost being killed a few times has put my life into pretty sharp focus. I don't care about money. I just don't think I could live without you anymore."

She gripped his arm.

"But how do I know that's true?" he said, turning away from her and facing the wall. "If I wasn't good enough before?"

"You were always good enough before," she said.

"But you don't understand. I'm fucking colorblind."

"I know," she said, rubbing his arm. "It doesn't matter. You just see the world differently."

"The critics will tear me to pieces when they figure it out, without all the distractions. And how am I supposed to follow this? I don't even know if I'll be able to paint like that anymore. Will you still love me when the money and fame fade away?"

It bothered her that she couldn't see his eyes. She sat up and pulled him back toward her.

"You've saved my life, Tom. I'm here now. You just have to believe me."

"I don't know. That pile of paintings just sold for $1.4 million." Tom bit his lip and smiled. "Are you a gold digger?" He laughed uneasily and stared ahead at the empty white wall.

"Shit. I'm gonna have to spend the rest of my life proving that I really love you, aren't I?" she murmured softly.

"Yep. But don't worry. I can think of a few ways you can make it up to me." He laughed and turned off the light.

ABOUT THE AUTHOR

K.B. Jensen is an author and journalist. *Painting with Fire* was her debut novel. As a former reporter, she has written extensively about crime in the Chicago suburbs. Jensen grew up in Minneapolis and currently lives in Chicago, with her husband, daughter and rescued border collie/lab mix. In her spare time she enjoys teaching downhill skiing and traveling the world.

Jensen's second novel, *A Storm of Stories*, published in 2016, handles love, craziness and impossibility. For more, visit www.kbjensenauthor.com.

Reviews are greatly appreciated. To connect with Jensen, visit facebook.com/kbjensenauthor, twitter.com/KB_Jensen or email kbjensen.author@gmail.com.

Made in the USA
Charleston, SC
25 March 2016